The Grub-and-Stakers Move a Mountain

By Alisa Craig

THE GRUB-AND-STAKERS MOVE A MOUNTAIN
A PINT OF MURDER

The Grub-and-Stakers Move a Mountain

ALISA CRAIG

PUBLISHED FOR THE CRIME CLUB BY

DOUBLEDAY & COMPANY, INC.

GARDEN CITY, NEW YORK

1981

The imaginary town of Lobelia Falls is supposed to be situated near the imaginary city of Scottsbeck, not very far from Lake Ontario. The author checked several reference sources to make sure no place of either name really exists. As the book is going to press, she has just learned that there is in fact a body of water known as Lobelia Lake in the Thunder Bay area, a long distance from her imagined locale. Needless to say, no connection between this story and any real town or inhabitant in the Lobelia Lake area should be drawn since the author didn't know such a place existed, has never been there, and still has no idea what it's like. If she had, she'd have thought up a different place-name and not have to be making this explanation.

She is at this point quite prepared to hear that a Grub-and-Stake Gardening and Roving Club also exists, and will be delighted to serve on the Tea Committee should its members care to invite her to a meeting. However, her intention has been to create a wholly fictitious set of characters, places, and events. Any resemblance to actual persons or situations is inadvertent and coincidental.

Library of Congress Cataloging in Publication Data

Craig, Alisa.
The grub-and-stakers move a mountain.

I. Title.
PS3553.R22G7   813'.54
ISBN: 0-385-17411-X
Library of Congress Catalog Card Number 80–2074

First Edition

For the Three Graces:
Grace, Grace, and, of course, Grace

The Grub-and-Stakers Move a Mountain

CHAPTER 1

"Whan that Aprille with his shoures soote," mused Dittany Henbit, spelling out the words in her mind as was her habit and no doubt getting at least one of them wrong as at least a dozen Aprilles had passed since her eighth-grade teacher had made her do that paper on Chaucer. The chief thrust of her argument, as she recalled, was that Chaucer wrote better than he spelled. Miss MacWilliams had sniffily penned, "Too bad you don't," under the undistinguished mark she'd awarded Dittany's effort.

There was no telling what Miss MacWilliams would have had to say about Arethusa Monk, whose latest effusion Dittany ought to have been at home in the shabbiest house on Applewood Avenue typing a final draft of at this precise point in time. Arethusa, who wrote strangely popular paperback novels of the "Ods bodikins, Sir Percy" school, was the best and the worst of clients, depending on whether it was worktime or paytime. Ten minutes ago, realizing that at least a hundred pages of egads and forsooths stood between her and any hope of a check, Dittany had shoved back her chair and headed for the great outdoors.

A person could stand only so much. One more impeccable Mechlin lace frill falling negligently over one more strong, shapely hand taking one more pinch of snuff from one more chased silver snuffbox with one more exquisitely limned ivory miniature of the beauteous but stupid Lady Ermintrude set into the lid, and Dittany would have been driven to od Sir Percy's bodikins once and for all. That was why she was sloshing through the slush and mud with a storm coat buttoned up to her ears, a wool cap on her head, and a quiver of arrows slung over her shoulder.

Very few people in Lobelia Falls went walking without their bows and arrows, not because of hostile tribes but on account of Minerva Oakes's grandmother. Winona Pitcher, as she then was, had been the first young woman from Lobelia Falls ever to attend a Female Academy of Higher Learning. During that era of ruffled corset covers and lawn sports for the gentry, archery had been all the vogue at the Academy, as tending to develop the feminine contours while keeping the ankles discreetly covered. When she returned to marry Mr. Oakes and lead the smart young social set in her home town, Winona had brought her enthusiasm with her and here it had taken root.

Roving, or strolling through the byways of which southern Ontario then had so many more than highways, and shooting at random targets was more fun than plugging away at standing archery butts, so Winona suggested forming a Lady Rovers' Club. Since everybody who cared to join was already a member of the Grub-and-Stake Garden Club, it was simpler to make a slight change in the existing bylaws and name. Husbands and sons snickered at the Grub-and-Stake Gardening and Roving Club but soon realized what they were missing and formed the Male Archers' Target and Game Shooting Association. Before long, Girl Guides and Boy Scouts were holding archery drill at every meeting. By now the sight of a tot barely out of diapers zipping an arrow bang into the gold was by no means uncommon in Lobelia Falls.

Today Dittany had no special intention of shooting. She'd simply picked up her bow and quiver as naturally as she'd put on her boots and mittens. That was the main advantage of being owner, manager, and sole employee of the Henbit Secretarial Service. One not only made a living of sorts, one could also get outdoors and draw a bow at a venture when one was, as Chaucer might have put it, Sir Percy'd yppe to ye eyeballes, although, come to think of it, Chaucer would likely have said so in a more forthrightly Chaucerian manner.

Dittany couldn't imagine what had started her on Chaucer all of a sudden, unless she was subliminally comparing Cat Alley, down which she was walking, to the sort of road over which old

Geoffrey's pilgrims would have slogged their loquacious way. Perhaps Cat Alley might look less like the wrong end of nowhere had this been in fact Aprille instead of the last week in March, but Dittany was inclined to think not. She knew the laggards who were supposed to take care of the lane, and a scurvier bunch of knaves even Arethusa Monk would be hard put to invent. Those monsters of depravity on the so-called Highway Department were no doubt too busy shoveling blacktop into the potholes on Rover's Row, where several town officials lived, to have any time or budget left for grading and oiling, much less paving, the route to her own favorite prowling ground.

Thus brooded Dittany Henbit on this lousy morning or afternoon as the case might be. Living alone as she had done since her widowed mother succumbed to the sales talk of a traveling representative in fashion eyewear, Dittany tended to lose track of the time. All she knew for sure was that it was still March and she was sick and tired of it. She was trying to recall something unflattering Chaucer had said about March when Ethel larruped out of the partly thawed swamp and planted a muddy paw on Dittany's best wool and camel-hair slacks, which she should have had sense enough not to wear in the first place because she might have known Ethel would come whoofling along sooner or later.

There was no telling what Chaucer would have said about Ethel. Probably something along the general lines of, "What in Goddes nayme ys thatte?"

Ethel was generally supposed to be part beagle, part bloodhound, part black bear and the rest a mystery although speculation ranged everywhere from badger to brontosaurus. The town clerk, insisting that she wear a dog license on the off chance that she did in fact happen to be a dog, classified her as "mixed breed," which was as close as anybody was apt to get.

Theoretically Ethel belonged to the Binkles, Dittany's neighbors, who'd got her from the dog pound on a charitable impulse they wished they hadn't had. However, they'd striven to do their duty. Henry Binkle had spent several weekends building a super-sized doghouse with stained glass windows. Jane Binkle had locked up chewable objects and tried to interest Ethel in a balanced diet. When it came to exercising her, they were licked before they started.

The Binkles were middle-aged, childless folk who owned a bookshop over at the shopping mall, about ten miles away. After a hard day among the Agatha Christies their notion of a pleasant evening was a leisurely game of chess with Ethel curled up beside them on the hearthrug. Ethel's own proclivities ran more along the lines of "Let us then be up and doing with a heart for any fate."

Ethel and Dittany had been soulmates from the start. On that fateful day when the Binkles brought the animal home from the pound, Dittany had happened to be sitting at the picnic table in her own back yard, eating a ham sandwich. Without waiting to be invited, Ethel had slipped her leash, leaped a five-foot hedge, and whisked the sandwich from Dittany's hand. As the Binkles stood aghast, Dittany had gone inside and made two more sandwiches, one with mustard for herself, one plain for Ethel.

Ethel loved to go roving with Dittany, and Dittany was seldom averse to following where Ethel's adventurous spirit led. It wasn't that Ethel had the better grasp of geography, it was just that both she and Dittany, like that lady friend of the late Mr. Wordsworth, preferred to dwell among th'untrodden ways. Off the beaten path, they were less apt to run into Arethusa Monk wandering along in a bemused state, muttering about Sir Percy and the lovely fathead to whom he was forever plighting his troth but never getting down to the nitty gritty because Arethusa's readers were much too high-minded to tolerate any goings-on.

Unfortunately the writer was never too lost in fantasy to stop Dittany and demand an opinion on whatever scene happened to be coursing through her luridly fecund mind at the moment. Since Dittany's bread and butter depended on her being tactful, evasive, and sometimes downright untruthful, such encounters were seldom fruitful and always upsetting. They only served as a reminder that ere long the Henbit Secretarial Service would be struggling with yet another fistful of illegibility.

Arethusa had a habit of snatching a page out of her typewriter in a frenzy of self-disgust, wadding it up, and chucking it into the wastebasket. There was no reason why she shouldn't, and often a perfectly sound reason why she should. The trouble was that Arethusa was apt to regret her impulse, fish out the wad, and try to press the paper smooth again under whatever weighty tome she was using for historical research; Arethusa's notion of research being to shut her eyes, open the book at random, stick a pin into the page, and insert whatever fact the pin happened to light on willy-nilly into the text.

Neither the pressing nor the pinning contributed much to the coherence of the manuscripts. Arethusa also forgot to number her pages more often than not and let her cat Rudolph, named for her pet villain, sleep in the box where she threw them. As Rudolph was a restless sleeper, the pages tended to get mixed up, clawed, and occasionally chewed. Dittany not only had to retype the ensuing mess, she had to make sense of it first. Only the facts that Arethusa made pots of money, paid lavishly on the dot, and was fun to be with when she could get her mind off Sir Percy made the struggle worth while.

This had been a particularly trying winter. Snowstorms and gales had kept Arethusa housebound, so the snuff and hair powder had piled up at a frightening rate. Dittany had been hard pressed to stay ahead of the fluttering fans, the swelling bosoms and coquettish glances. She particularly didn't want to meet Arethusa today because Arethusa would be sure to ask how she was getting on with the current opus in which Lady Ermintrude was about to become enmeshed in the perfidious toils of an evil baronet, Rudolph being away on vacation. Dittany would then (a) have to confess that she was playing hooky and be called a caitiff knave or possibly even a base varlet or (b) make believe the work was going great guns and then be expected to produce a sheaf of finished typescript she didn't have.

She could always pretend Ethel had eaten it. Ethel probably would, if asked. At the moment, Ethel was cavorting up Cat Alley toward the Enchanted Mountain. Dittany ran after her. Despite the bluster March was trying to get out of its system before April came along and put a damper on its fun, despite the chill and the slop and the fact that her best pair of slacks was probably ruined forever, it felt good to be out here with the wind whipping her nose, no doubt, to a piquant shade of scarlet. Nevertheless, Dittany was glad when they got into the lee of the Enchanted Mountain.

Nobody remembered who had given this not really very impressive lump of glacial detritus its fanciful name, or why. Approximately a century ago, two bachelor brothers named Hunneker, skedaddlers from somewhere down in the States, had decided to return to their native heath, now that the Civil War was well over, and become carpetbaggers. Because they couldn't find a buyer for the real estate they'd acquired during their stay in Canada, they magnanimously deeded it over to the then embryonic town of Lobelia Falls, and because they couldn't think of any use to which it might be put, they had vaguely stated that the land was to be used for the common weal.

Needless to say, the rugged individualists of Lobelia Falls had never achieved a meeting of the minds as to where their common weal lay. As a result, nobody had done anything. Over the past century the Enchanted Mountain had become a refuge for all sorts of growing things that had been developed out of existence elsewhere.

Here could be found the Pointed-Leaved Tick Trefoil (*Desmodium glutinosum*) along with the showier *Desmodium canadense* and the naughty *Desmodium nudiflorum*. Here flourished the demure *Silene antirrhina* or Sleepy Catchfly, as well as the Heart-leaved Twayblade (*Listera cordata*). Here also proliferated that unpopular thornless trifoliate *Rhus toxicodendron*, or Poison Ivy, which was a major reason why the Enchanted Mountain was not a more frequented place, except by Dittany, Ethel, and a few intrepid souls of like enthusiasms.

As Conservation Committee chairman of the Grub-and-Stake Gardening and Roving Club, Dittany had got into the habit of considering the Enchanted Mountain not only her private playground but also her personal responsibility. She was therefore horror-stricken to find the place infested on this unlikely morning by a large man steering a backhoe straight toward the only patch of Spotted Pipsissewa in Lobelia Township.

After one startled, anguished glance, Dittany charged like a tigress into the maw of the oncoming machine. "Get away from that Spotted Pipsissewa!" she shrieked.

The operator looked up in surprise, as well he might, and stalled his motor. However, he immediately tried to start it again so Dittany called up her ultimate weapon.

"Ethel, sick him!"

Ethel hadn't the remotest idea what "Sick him" meant, but she was always glad to make a new acquaintance. Baying in delight, she clambered aboard the backhoe.

The man made the grave mistake of standing up. He proved to be even larger than Dittany had thought, but Ethel was bigger still. She draped her front paws over his shoulders and began licking his face with a tongue the size of a bath mat. He staggered backward, lost his balance, and landed unhurt in the soft mud. Assuming this was the next move in whatever game they'd begun to play, Ethel sat down on his chest and flailed him joyously about the hips and thighs with her powerful tail.

"Call off your whatever-it-is," he gasped.

Under other circumstances Dittany might have obliged, for the man was not uncomely of countenance or much further advanced in years than she. As it was, she hardened her heart.

"She's not mine. Ethel, stay! Don't move until this—this *person* explains what he's doing up here with that ghastly backhoe. This happens to be town property, in case you don't know, mister."

"And I happen to be a town employee."

With a mighty heave, the operator managed to unseat Ethel, flinging her on her back in the mire and sending her into fresh ecstasies. He got to his feet and began picking last year's oak leaves out of his rather attractive red-brown curls. "I'm here to do percolation tests."

"Why?"

"To see how fast the water drains off," he explained with remarkable forbearance, all things considered.

"I know what a perk test is, thank you. I meant why are you doing them here?"

"Because my boss told me to. Look, ma'am—er, miss, there's nothing to get excited about."

"That's what you think. Get that backhoe off this mountain within twenty seconds or I'll put you under citizens' arrest for vandalism."

"On what grounds, eh?" The man wiped his muddy hand on his shirt, pulled a map out of his pocket, and planted a far from dainty forefinger on a diagram of what was officially known and thereon designated as the Hunneker Land Grant. "We're here, right?"

"Wrong," said Dittany. "I mean we are but you've no business to be."

"You'll have to take that up with Mr. Architrave. He said he'd meet me here, though I haven't seen him yet."

"That figures." Dittany knew Mr. Architrave of old. He'd been around almost as long as the mountain, squat and stubborn and thickheaded, holding on as head of the Water Department by sheer cussedness years after he should have been retired from a position he'd never been capable of filling in the first place. He was always having to hire new men because nobody could stand him long. This must be the latest.

"Anyway," the operator went on, "yesterday afternoon he gave me this plot plan and told me to bring the backhoe up here today and do a perk test wherever you see one of those red dots. And you're standing on one of my dots right now so I'm afraid I'll have to ask you to move, eh?"

"You can ask till your teeth fall out and a fat lot of good it'll do you. Nobody's said anything to me about red dots, and I'm chairman of the Conservation Committee. We don't need perk tests up here, we need a few gallons of poison ivy spray and some wood chips to make paths with. Those should come from Mr. Schwunder of the Highway Department. I suppose Schwunder got the bright idea of passing the buck to the Water Department and knew he'd get away with it because Mr. Architrave is solid caramel custard from the neck up, and always was.

Please go away, Mr. Whatever-your-name-is. I'm sure that old nincompoop has made another of his bloopers and you could do irreparable damage to some very rare wildflowers if you start messing around up here. Haven't you something else to do?"

"We do seem to have quite a backlog of work," he admitted. "Mr. Architrave was giving me a pep talk yesterday about getting caught up."

"I'm sure he was. He'd rather talk than work any day. Architrave ought to be running the Great Glacier instead of the Water Department. How long have you been working for him, eh?"

"Just since yesterday morning. And I'm not all that keen to get fired my second day out for disobeying orders, if you don't mind."

"Why not? You'll be leaving soon anyway. Everybody who's halfway competent quits after a week or two of screaming frustration and the rest come down with sleeping sickness."

"If he's all that incompetent, why do you keep him on?"

"Because he's the only person in town who knows where the water mains are. He won't map them because he's just barely smart enough to realize he'd be out on his ear like a shot if he did. So now that you've heard about the birds and the bees, why don't you pick up your toys and go play somewhere else? This is a stupid time to be doing perk tests anyway. The ground's soaking wet on top and frozen solid underneath. You couldn't possibly get a true reading."

"I did ask Mr. Architrave about that," he admitted, "but—"

"But he hemmed and hawed and started to bluster, which should have tipped you off right then and there. He'd got his wires crossed somehow and was ashamed to say so. Once he finds out where he went wrong he'll weasel out from under and blame you, so why don't you stop while you're still ahead?"

"I had an awful time getting this backhoe up here," he muttered.

Dittany looked down at the churned-up track the machine had left. "Yes, and you ran right through the Plantain-leaved Pussytoes. Look, do you see that big boulder over there?"

"Clearly and distinctly. What about it?"

"You start up that ugly mess of metal, eh, and head straight as a die for that boulder. When you get exactly three feet beyond the ash tree—"

"Which is the ash tree?"

"What did they teach you in percolation school, for heaven's sake? How can anybody not know what an ash tree looks like?"

"I know perfectly well what an ash tree looks like. They have bunches of orange berries on them. And you can pick off a twig and use it to keep witches away," he added with a thoughtful inflection that Dittany chose to ignore. "They have feather-compound leaves, visible buds, and no glands."

"They don't have leaves in March," she replied primly, "nor do they have orange berries because the birds ate them over the winter. So why don't you leave your rotten old backhoe sitting there till the buds come out and the glands don't, eh? Then you'll know where to—"

"Get down!"

The man from the Water Department flung Dittany behind him as an arrow whizzed through the air and buried itself in the ash tree. She screamed, partly from shock, partly because she'd landed against something hard and sharp on the backhoe. Ethel began to bay and the man to yell.

"Hey, you over there! Watch where you're shooting."

Dittany stared up at the long shaft, still quivering from its impact with the tree. "That's a hunting arrow," she said shakily. "It could kill a moose."

"If we'd been a few steps closer, it could have gone straight through the pair of us," said her protector even more shakily. "What the hell kind of town is this, anyhow? You all carry bows and arrows like Robin Hood and his merry murderers. Do you take pot shots at each other for fun, or what?"

"No." Dittany wet her lips. "We're drilled from the cradle up never to shoot unless we're sure of a clear target. We never have accidents."

"Then maybe this was no accident, eh? Look, Miss—"

"Henbit," she replied automatically. "Dittany Henbit."

"Miss Henbit, I don't know about you but I'm either mad as hell or scared as hell, and I'm not sure which. I'm going to have a look over that ridge. Can you hold the dog back here?"

"I'll try. Be careful."

Dittany clung to Ethel's collar and watched him crawl forward, using whatever cover he could find, until he disappeared over the top of the ridge. No other arrow followed, and she let out her breath at last in an immense sigh of relief. That must have been simply a wild shot, then the bowman would have heard the yelling and barking and held fire. But why hadn't he or she heard them earlier, arguing over the backhoe? The shot couldn't have come from far away or the arrow wouldn't have penetrated the tree so deeply.

Ethel whimpered, and Dittany took a firmer grip on her collar. The dog was being oddly well behaved, now she thought of it. Normally Ethel would have gone bounding up to a hunter and spoiled his shot if she'd got the chance. Why hadn't she done so this time? Either she'd been too interested in the argument over the backhoe, or the wind hadn't carried the hunter's scent over the ridge, or else she'd recognized it as that of somebody she knew and disliked. Ethel had a few unfavorite people, and with those she could be remarkably snooty.

The arrow had stopped jiggling. Dittany scrutinized the shaft and was surprised to see a solid inch-wide black band above the feathers. Everybody who shot in and around Lobelia Falls had some sort of mark on his or her arrows to distinguish them from anyone else's. They all knew each other's marks in the same way that one lobsterman knows another's pots by the shape and color of the buoys. Dittany's, for example, had a narrow band of pale green next to the feathers to show she was a member of the Grub-and-Stake, and three rings of pale blue above it. The pale blue identified her as a Henbit and the three rings indicated that she was the third generation of her family to belong to the club. In some families the marks got far more complicated, but they were easy enough to read when one knew the code. Never in her life, though, had she seen such a simple, ominous mark as this. A hunting arrow shot from a bow with a 65-pound pull could be a deadlier weapon than a rifle bullet. That one black band made her very uncomfortable indeed.

The man from the Water Department was gone what seemed like an awfully long time. Dittany, more uneasy by the moment, was inching her way out from behind the backhoe and wondering how insane she'd be to go and look for him when he came stumbling over the ridge, his face a ghastly mask.

"What happened?" she cried. "Did you see who shot the arrow?"

"No." He sat down on a stump and wiped a shaking hand across his mouth. "I saw Mr. Architrave. Pinned to the ground. With an arrow clean through him, back to front. Excuse me, I think I'm going to be—"

He was. At last the sounds of distress from behind the backhoe ceased and he came back, wiping his face again.

"Sorry," he muttered. "Didn't know I was such a sissy. Miss Henbit, you'll have to go for the police, eh? Take the dog just in case."

"You're not staying here alone?"

"What else can I do? It's not right to leave him."

"But what if the archer comes back?"

His face twisted into a wry attempt at a grin. "That'll be my tough luck, won't it? For God's sake, could you hurry?"

CHAPTER 2

Luckily no place was far from any other place in Lobelia Falls. Three minutes and twenty-seven seconds after she'd left the Enchanted Mountain, Dittany was at the police station, panting out her story to Sergeant MacVicar.

"And you say John Architrave is lying on that bleak mountainside pierced through the heart by an arrow black and dire," said the sergeant, who sometimes beguiled the duller stretches by reading Arethusa Monk's books.

"I said Mr. Architrave was dead," Dittany replied. "I don't know what part of him the arrow went through because that man from the Water Department didn't tell me and I'm only assuming it had a wide black band around the shaft because the one that almost hit us did."

"But nobody's arrow has a black band around the shaft," said Sergeant MacVicar. He was a past president of the Male Archers' Target and Game Shooting Association and ought to know if anyone did.

"Somebody's does because if I'd been two feet taller it might have parted my hair for me," Dittany insisted. "Don't you think we ought to get back there as fast as we can?"

"M'yes, that would appear to be the judicious course. If you'll excuse me, I'll just ask Mrs. MacVicar to step in and mind the phone."

This was no big deal since the police station was situated in what might otherwise have been the MacVicars' front parlor. Mrs. MacVicar entered, having first shed her apron, for she was punctilious about maintaining the dignity of her husband's office, shook her neat and comely head, and urged all speed as naturally she was avid for further information.

"Some hunter from the States, no doubt," was her theory. Mrs. MacVicar tended to lay any local disruption of law and order to hunters from the States, of whom in fact Lobelia Falls had very few. "And you say it was Minerva Oakes's boarder who found him?"

"I said it was a new man from the Water Department," Dittany replied in surprise. "I've no idea where he lives. I don't even know his name."

"Frankland," said Mrs. MacVicar promptly. "Tall, broad-shouldered chap about thirty years old with an affable though somewhat unpolished manner. Curly reddish-brown hair, blue eyes, ruddy complexion, clean-shaven—"

"And a weak stomach," Dittany finished to show she wasn't entirely unobservant. "He was being sick all over the mountain."

"Ah, well, your average layman is not hardened to vile atrocities," said Sergeant MacVicar as if he were in the habit of finding bodies on the station doorstep with the morning paper. "Mother, see if you can get hold of Dr. Peagrim and explain that he's wanted up there as soon as possible. We'll be on the lookout for him."

He accoutered himself with handcuffs and a number of other things he couldn't imaginably need, bowed Dittany into the police car, and off they roared, although not very far, as it was necessary to get out and walk once they reached the periphery of the Hunneker Land Grant. Frankland ran down to meet them, looking a shade less green by now, and managed to lead Sergeant MacVicar to the corpse without further upheaval. Both men appeared to take it for granted Dittany would either go on home or cower beside the backhoe, but she tagged along a discreet step or two in the rear, wishing she hadn't been quite so rude about the now demised Mr. Architrave.

When she saw the form spread-eagled on the ground, though, she lost any sense of personal concern. It simply wasn't real, that fat black dummy with the black-banded shaft sticking out a few inches between the shoulder blades.

"John was a heavy-set man and he has on a thick overcoat," mused Sergeant MacVicar, "yet the arrow went through him like a hot knife through butter. That was not done with a dainty lady's bow." He smiled a bit at the one Dittany was still carrying, though in fact it was no paltry weapon. "A hunting bow with at least a 65-pound pull and probably more, I should say. It would take a strong man to draw that."

"Not necessarily," Dittany started to argue. "I know some women who—" She shut up. This was no time to advertise any friend's prowess.

"And you saw no sign of anybody, Mr. Frankland, if I am correct in calling you so?" the sergeant inquired politely.

"That's right, Frankland. Most people call me Ben. No, the only sign of life I saw was that arrow that just missed us over by the backhoe. I expect Miss Henbit told you about that, eh?"

"Yes, she did, and where is the arrow now?"

"It's still in the ash tree," Dittany replied. "It went in pretty deep. I noticed because I'm so used to chasing arrows," she half apologized because after all it had been rather brave of Ben Frankland to go over that ridge not knowing what he'd find, even if he perhaps hadn't then realized how dangerous a longbow can be.

Sergeant MacVicar shook his head. "Anybody who shoots no better than that has no business out here. What puzzles me is why he shot more than once. Did you make no outcry?"

"I yelled my bloody head off when that arrow zinged past us," said Frankland.

"And Ethel barked and I'm sure I must have screamed," Dittany added. "We hadn't been exactly silent beforehand, either. We were having a few words about whether he should be digging up the wildflowers."

"Ah," said Sergeant MacVicar. "Then it would seem that the miscreant shot poor old John first, by accident or so we must piously hope. Hearing voices in the distance, he then loosed a second arrow in the hope of frightening you off so that he could escape unseen."

"But why bother? We never dreamed Mr. Architrave had

been shot. If it hadn't been for that other arrow coming at us, we wouldn't have known anybody else was up here."

"John may have cried out when he was struck."

"If he did, we didn't hear him."

"Ah, but the bowman would not know that, would he? Being on the opposite side of the ridge, eh, he would have heard John more loudly and you more softly, if you catch the drift of my argument. It would not occur to him that with you the reverse would be true. The only other explanation that occurs to me is that the hunter never knew he'd hit John and was merely shooting at random for practice, which it would appear he sorely needed. But in that case, why did he not go looking for his arrows?"

There was an uncomfortable little silence. The three of them looked at each other, then Sergeant MacVicar said in a firm departmental tone, "In any event it was none of our folk. Nobody in Lobelia Falls has arrows like these."

"If you want my opinion for what it's worth," said Frankland, "it was some drunk who came up off the highway."

He gestured at the ribbon of asphalt that stretched from the back side of the Hunneker Land Grant toward the distant horizon with nothing to break the monotony but a farmhouse or two. "Probably saw what looked like a deserted area and thought he'd get in a spot of quiet poaching. Mr. Architrave had said he'd meet me here, as I mentioned to Miss Henbit, and I'd been wondering where he was. It must have been just that he came up one side of the ridge while I was on the other. With that squatty build and his black overcoat, I suppose a person might have mistaken him for a black bear if they didn't look too hard, eh?"

Sergeant MacVicar nodded profoundly. "That might well happen."

"So the hunter could have shot him sort of accidentally on purpose as you might say, then maybe got excited and let off a wild shot just for the heck of it, heard us yelling and realized what he'd done, and hightailed it out of here."

"You did not hear a car drive off?"

"Not that I recall, but we mightn't have noticed with the

highway not all that far away. Anyway, Miss Henbit and I were both sort of in shock for a second there, I guess, after that arrow came at us. Then we chewed the fat about her holding the dog while I went to see what was up, and I took my time getting over the ridge, I don't mind telling you. I was none too keen on stopping another of those arrows like the tree did. And when I spotted Mr. Architrave, I—well, it hit me right in the guts, if you want to know. I guess I didn't put up much of a show as a hero, eh? Anyhow, as soon as I could pull myself together, I went back and asked Miss Henbit to go for the police."

"As was right and proper," said Sergeant MacVicar. "This is exactly how you found John? You didn't try to move him?"

"God, no!" Frankland mopped his face again. "I wouldn't have touched him with a ten-foot pole. I could see there was nothing to be done, though I suppose we should have got a doctor anyway."

"A call is out for Dr. Peagrim," Sergeant MacVicar replied rather grandly. "If Mrs. Stumm has not started her twins, he should be along any time now. Your theory has merit, Mr. Frankland. I shall examine the terrain for clues. It would be advisable for you to suspend any further activity in the area for the time being."

"Yes, but what's this activity for?" cried Dittany. "Mr. Architrave gave Mr. Frankland a plot plan with red dots on it where leaching tests were supposed to be done. Can you imagine why?"

Sergeant MacVicar pondered, then shook his majestic head. "I cannot. John explained nothing to you, Mr. Frankland?"

"No, just told me to bring the backhoe up here and dig where the dots were. I figured it wasn't my place to ask questions, being new on the job. I thought maybe he'd tell me when he met me here. Say, you know, he must have heard me trying to jockey that darned backhoe up the slope. I wonder why he didn't come over. Of course he wouldn't have known which spot I meant to dig at first. See, he'd given me this plot plan."

Frankland pulled out the map of the Hunneker Land Grant for MacVicar's inspection. "I was just starting to work on this spot here when Miss Henbit came along and told me I was acting in violation of the Conservation Committee so I decided I'd better lay off till I'd made sure I wasn't in the wrong place, though I didn't see how I could be. If Mr. Architrave had come over I could have checked with him. Might have saved his life, eh?"

Sergeant MacVicar perched a pair of gold-rimmed spectacles on the impressive Highland sweep of his nose and studied the map. "You were apparently at the indicated place, but I am as puzzled as Dittany with regard to John's reason for sending you here. Mrs. MacVicar's Cousin Maude's oldest son Clinton has endeavored without success ever since last June to get a percolation test done on some land he wants to build on and others have similar tales of woe stemming from John's dilatory habits. You must know, Mr. Frankland, that, while Lobelia Falls has thus far rejected a town sewer as being pretentious and citified, we are very strict about proper septage and leaching beds. Percolation tests are an essential prelude to any construction project, but as no construction would ever be planned up here, John's reason for ordering these particular tests eludes me. I am reluctantly forced to the conclusion that poor old John, whom we have always valued more for the rectitude of his character than for the strength of his intellect, had finally, as my irreverent grandson would put it, popped his cork. Dittany, would you be good enough to explain to the ladies at the club that Mrs. MacVicar is unavoidably detained on official business?"

"Oh my gosh!" gasped Dittany. "What time is it?"

"Half past two. You are on the Tea Committee this month, and you have already been late twice in a row."

Sergeant MacVicar's cork, at least, was firmly in place. Dittany sped for Applewood Avenue without even pausing to say good-by.

CHAPTER 3

The house on Applewood Avenue had become Dittany's more or less by default when her mother remarried and moved to Vancouver. Her new stepfather had offered to include his wife's only offspring in a package deal, but Dittany had refused. She was very fond of Bert, but she had no desire to move.

Whereas the former Mrs. Henbit had always been a goer, Dittany herself was a natural-born stayer. Lobelia Falls was where she belonged. From the time she could remember, she had participated wholeheartedly in community life. At five years of age she'd pranced around the kindergarten's field day maypole with a pair of pink crepe paper butterfly wings pinned to her yellow organdie back. At eight she'd marched with the Brownies in the Dominion Day parade. At eleven she'd picked up discarded Molson's Ale bottles and Hatfield's Potato Chip wrappers for six hours without a break during the Girl Guides' Annual Roadside Cleanup Day. At fifteen she'd whanged a mean glockenspiel in the regional high school band.

Dittany had been proud and honored to join the Grub-and-Stake Gardening and Roving Club as a third-generation member. She'd honestly meant to be a credit to the organization but she was, after all, her mother's daughter and the former Mrs. Henbit's best-laid plans tended to gang agley as often as not.

This had been one of those agley days. Dittany had started out to be beautifully organized. She'd remembered she was on the Tea Committee even before Mrs. MacVicar called to remind her. She'd prepared dainty sandwiches on thin-sliced date bread, filled with cream cheese and walnuts plus a dash of horseradish for zest and a sprinkling of paprika for color. She'd trimmed the crusts, carved her creations into neat triangles, and packed them between layers of biodegradable waxed paper in a Crawford's biscuit tin. She'd set the tin in the fridge to keep the sandwiches fresh.

She'd washed her hair and fluffed it with one of the four blow-dryers her mother had bought her in moments of forgetful benevolence. She'd thought of plucking her eyebrows but quit after a couple of experimental tweaks because Dittany was no masochist. Anyway they were so light a brown they didn't show much. Dittany's coloring was all betwixt and between: her hair more blondish than brownish, her eyes more green than blue, her complexion more fair than not, more peachy than pinky. Her face might never have launched a thousand ships, especially not on Lake Ontario, but it was a face most people would rather see than not.

She'd got herself slicked up in the aforementioned camel-hair slacks and a matching cashmere pullover, being small and slim enough to wear such garments without bulging except where she was supposed to bulge. She'd added Gram Henbit's gold chain and watch, which didn't tell time anymore but was quite lovely to look at. Then she realized she'd done all these things hours too soon, so she'd dutifully sat down to stap Sir Percy's buttons until she couldn't stand that any longer. Then she'd gone for that catastrophic walk and now here she was with pawprints all over her clothes and huge questions in her mind and no time to do anything about either.

She dashed into the house, grabbed her biscuit tin, and raced to the public library where meetings were now held since one member had resigned in a huff because she was forever being asked to have the group at her house and another had quit because she never got asked at all. She arrived one step ahead of the lecturer who was to present a program, with colored slides, on Larkspur and Lepidoptera, and flung herself into the tiny, inconvenient kitchen.

There she found Caroline Pitz scowling into the recalcitrant recesses of a thirty-cup coffeemaker and Ellie Despard refilling the teakettle at what everybody had complained since the day it was installed was a grossly inadequate sink. Samantha Burberry was arranging lemon squares on a Crown Derby plate.

"Sorry I'm late," Dittany panted. "I've been having the most fantastically ghastly experience."

"When have you ever not?" drawled Samantha. "I hope you've brought sandwiches. Imogene Laplace was supposed to and she made these gorgeous lemony things instead. Not that I wouldn't rather have them myself"—she suited deed to word by helping herself to one then and there—"but it says in the bylaws we're supposed to have sandwiches."

Even with her mouth full of lemon square Samantha managed to sound coolly amused, although she herself was chairman of the Legislative Committee and would be first to pounce on any infringement of the club's constitution.

"Yes, I made sandwiches," sighed Dittany. Realizing it would be futile to try telling her wild story now, she reached for another serving plate and began unpacking her goodies with a steady rhythm born of much practice. "Goodness knows what they taste like."

Samantha, having dispatched the lemon square, reached for one of the tiny triangles and nibbled with epicurean discernment. "Delicious," she pronounced. Samantha had the remarkable faculty of being able to put away any amount of food without adding an inch to her tall svelteness. More remarkably still, nobody hated her for it. Esprit de corps was high among the Grub-and-Stakers, though never so high as to make things dull.

Certainly the next half hour was anything but monotonous for Dittany. She ran her legs off bringing more sandwiches, more cream, more pastries to the tea table. She pestered the long-suffering library assistants for the loan of an extension cord so the lecturer could plug in her slide projector. What with one thing and another, she herself didn't get any tea until the meeting had started, the Tea Committee were washing up the last of the cups, and there was absolutely nothing left to eat but some sandwiches Zilla Trott had made.

Zilla's donations were seldom popular. Today's offerings were composed, as far as Dittany could determine, of wheat germ, grated raw parsnips, and homemade yogurt on bread made from oat hulls and cardboard. Having missed lunch, she ate them anyway and slipped into the meeting just in time to hear President Therese Boulanger ask, "And now is there any further business to discuss before I turn the meeting over to our Honorable Program Chairman?"

Without in the least intending to, Dittany bounded to her feet. "The Conservation Committee wishes to inquire whether any member knows why the late Mr. Architrave ordered percolation tests done on the Enchanted Mountain."

"Perk tests? *Late* Mr. Architrave?" An excited gabble swept around the room. Therese thumped her gavel mightily.

"Dittany, I'm sure we all want to know what's happened to Mr. Architrave. Could you tell us very briefly?"

"He was apparently shot by an out-of-town hunter who mistook him for a bear coming over the mountain."

She hadn't meant to be funny, but a few people giggled hysterically. Therese thumped again. "Now can anybody give us a specific answer to Dittany's question about the perk tests?"

Nobody could.

"Would someone care to make a motion that the Conservation Committee look into the matter and report its findings at the next meeting?"

"I so move," said Zilla Trott.

"Second the motion," said Samantha Burberry.

There wasn't a nay in the crowd.

"I further move," Zilla Trott went on, "that we get off our tails and start doing something to protect the wildflowers up there instead of sitting around saying we ought to as we've been doing for the past umpteen years, before some idiot does real harm on the mountain."

The ayes had it again. "And now," said Therese in a voice that brooked no opposition, parliamentary or otherwise, "I shall turn the meeting over to our Honorable Program Chairman."

The speaker was formally introduced. The lights were dimmed. The slide projector was twiddled until it achieved a sharp enough focus to satisfy all but the really picky. The lecture began.

No doubt about it, this lady knew her butterflies. Her slides were gorgeous, her delivery informative and amusing. Nevertheless Dittany viewed the Spangled Fritillary and the Zebra Swallowtail with a lackluster eye. She found her mind wandering from the Early Hairstreak and decided after due reflection that anybody who wanted her share of the Little Wood Nymph was welcome to it. She wished she'd kept her mouth shut about Mr. Architrave because she knew everybody would be pouncing on her like a Monarch on a milkweed as soon as the show was over. Before the Eastern Tailed Blue had waved its azure wings in farewell she was on her feet, ready to grab her biscuit tin and flee.

Then Hazel Munson stepped quietly into her way and murmured, "Can I give you a lift?"

This apparently commonplace offer stopped Dittany dead in her tracks. Hazel Munson knew perfectly well Dittany didn't need a lift and Hazel was not one to put herself forward. Without hesitation Dittany climbed into Hazel's car, slammed the door, and said, "Okay, what are you going to tell me that you don't want anyone else to hear?"

Hazel chuckled. "I thought I was being subtle. Let's get out of here first." She gunned her motor and swung around the corner. "I don't know if there's anything in this or not but, anyway, we had the Strephs over to dinner last night. They'd just got back from skiing in the Laurentians and naturally they wanted to tell us about their trip."

Dittany nodded. The Strephs and the Munsons were always doing strenuous things either separately or together.

"Anyway," Hazel went on, "while I was cutting the pie, Jim Streph said out of a clear blue sky, 'Don't you think it would be great to have maybe five or six really nice homes up on the Enchanted Mountain?' Dittany, I tell you I sat there with the pie knife in my hand and my mouth hanging open. Then I blurted out, 'No, I think it would be awful!'"

"So Jim didn't say any more and Margery asked for another cup of coffee, which surprised me very much because she always claims coffee keeps her awake. Though after the time she and I were sharing a tent and two raccoons got to fighting outside and she snored through the whole rumpus, I personally doubt if anything could."

"In other words, she was trying to change the subject?"

Hazel shrugged. "Margery doesn't go in much for tact as a rule. She's more for letting it all hang out, as the kids say. But if she thought Jim's career might be involved—it sounds silly talking like this. I don't know why I'm wasting your time."

"Hazel, you're not. Jim Streph is an architect, isn't he? Hasn't he done some work for Andy McNasty?"

"Why, yes. He's designed four or five of those development tracts for McNaster Construction. Oh, Dittany! Look, maybe you'd better invite me in for a cup of tea, not that I need it but somebody's sure to come along and see us talking like this and, after all, the Strephs are good friends of ours."

"Consider yourself invited. I could use something myself."

Hazel wiggled her somewhat too generous bosom out from behind the steering wheel, followed Dittany into the shabby roost of the Henbits, and headed for the tapestry-covered spring rocker everybody always tried to grab before somebody else beat them to it. As she plumped herself down, they heard a dismal, "Aw-oo!" from the rear of the house.

"That's just Ethel wanting her snack," Dittany explained. "She and I generally have tea and dog biscuits about now. I have the tea and she gets the biscuits. Hold on a second, will you? If I don't shut her up, she'll sit there and howl till the Binkles come home."

Dittany sped kitchenward. The howling stopped. Moments later she was back with a tray bearing a bottle, two glasses, and a plate of sweet meal biscuits. "She gets bored, poor thing. I thought we might as well open the last of the sherry Bert gave me at Christmas when he and Mum were here. I've been saving it for an emergency and if this isn't one, tell me what is, eh?"

Hazel took a sip. "It's lovely," she pronounced, but not with untrammeled joy. "Dittany, you don't honestly think McNaster would try to steal the Enchanted Mountain?"

"After what he did to the Hendryx place?" Dittany took her own glass and curled up on the grape-carved sofa where she always sat if she had to be polite about the rocker. "Hazel, you know as well as I what that man's capable of. He bought that lovely old house before anybody else even knew it was up for sale, and had it torn down that very same night. Nobody knew a thing till we heard the crashing and banging and by then it was too late to stop him."

"I know. And then what did he do but level off the lot and blacktop it to make more parking for the inn. That used to be such a nice place. Since he took it over, it's nothing but a honky-tonk. And he never got a variance for the parking lot or a permit to demolish the house, which ought to have been preserved in the first place because it was one of the finest buildings in town."

"And furthermore," Dittany snarled, "those exit and entrance signs are still sitting on town property even though McNaster was served with a writ to remove them ten months ago, and why?"

"Because he's got the darn town council in his pocket, that's why," said Hazel, letting Dittany refill her glass without even murmuring, "I shouldn't be drinking this at all, I'm too fat already," which showed what sort of state she was in. "But how could McNaster possibly get his grubby claws on the Enchanted Mountain? The Hunnekers deeded the land to the town in perpetuity. There's simply no way."

"Oh yeah?" snorted Dittany. "What do you bet McNaster's already convinced the Development Commission that the common weal would best be served by turning the grant into tax-producing private building lots? Why else would Jim Streph be talking about nice houses up there? Why else would Architrave send a new man who wouldn't be expected to know any better up there to do perk tests? Hazel, I still haven't told you what really happened about Mr. Architrave."

Dittany proceeded to do so. Hazel's pleasant brown eyes grew wider and wider, her gasps more frequent. "Well, I never!" was her verdict. "I don't see how you had the nerve to stay there. I'd have hightailed it for home and crawled under the bed. What makes you so sure it was a hunter?"

"Who said I was sure? I said this man Frankland said it must have been a hunter and Sergeant MacVicar said that was a reasonable theory but you never know what Sergeant MacVicar's really thinking till it's about half a second too late. Anyway, it can't have been McNaster who shot him because he's the lousiest shot in town and poor old Architrave was drilled through the middle of the back as neatly as—as I could have done it myself," Dittany finished in a sort of horrified whisper.

"Pooh," said Hazel. "You couldn't kill anybody. You even threw a kitten fit when you found out Minerva Oakes was shooting those squirrels that had chewed their way into her attic."

"Well, I must say I'd never have thought it of Minerva. Anyway, I have an alibi because I was with that Frankland man when the other arrow came over the ridge and plunked itself in the tree. And he has one because he was with me, and Mr. Architrave—Hazel, what am I talking about?"

"You're having a delayed reaction, that's all. Perfectly natural. Take a little more sherry. No, not for me, thanks. I won't be able to find the stove to get supper as it is. You know, Dittany, I was just thinking. I read an Agatha Christie once where somebody was supposed to have shot somebody from a blowgun only it turned out he'd stuck in the poisoned dart with his hand instead. Why couldn't McNaster have sneaked up behind John Architrave and—"

"Hazel, the arrow went clean through his body and stuck out in front far enough to pin him to the ground. You couldn't stab anybody that hard with an arrow, not just holding it in your hand. It's not like one of those rapiers Arethusa's always pinking the bad guy with, where there'd be a long, thin, sharp-pointed steel blade with a handle you could get a good grip on. Wait a second. I'll get an arrow and you try to stab me."

"Dittany, you're drunk! What if I succeeded? Go down cellar and fetch a pumpkin."

"I don't have a pumpkin. Would you settle for a squash?"

"A squash wouldn't be fair. They have awfully tough skins."

"So did old man Architrave. Besides, he was wearing his overcoat and I don't know what all underneath. A cardigan and a heavy shirt and a winter undershirt at least, wouldn't you think? I'm telling you, Hazel, it wouldn't work. Your hand would simply slide down the shaft. You'd have to take a hammer and pound the arrow in, and who's going to stand still for that?"

"I'll bet your hand wouldn't slip if you grabbed the arrow around the feathers."

"You'd mash the feathers all to heck, though, and these were standing up stiff and straight as you please. Gray ones. Do you think I wouldn't have noticed? Besides, what about that arrow that hit the ash tree? It was sticking in at least three inches, and I defy anybody to throw an arrow that far and make it stick. Actually, those were two remarkably good shots for anybody to make by accident, even with a heavy bow."

"All right, Dittany, I grant you the bow." Hazel nibbled thoughtfully at a sweet meal biscuit. "So if it wasn't an accident, what was the sense of shooting at the backhoe man? This Frankland was doing the perk tests he wanted, wasn't he?"

"He who?"

"McNaster, of course, if he's after the land."

"But so was Architrave. I mean, Mr. Architrave was the one who told Frankland to do them, so he had to be on McNaster's side, didn't he? Hazel, I'd adore to pin a deliberate murder on that scaly scaledrell. I mean scouny—oh, heck! That scurvy scur. Anyway, I wish we could, but I don't see how. Besides, McNaster's arrows have red and yellow stripes with purple feathers as you might expect from somebody who's got a taste like a can of worms. This was a single inch-wide stripe of solid black."

"Nobody has an inch-wide stripe of solid black."

"Everybody knows that. That's why they're talking about a hunter from the States."

"Then I daresay they're right and this is just one of those awful coincidences," sighed Hazel. "It's a mercy poor old John didn't wind up stuffed and mounted on somebody's mantelpiece. But I still say McNaster's morally responsible, for having got him up there in the first place. That is, assuming we're right in what we're assuming," she added, for Hazel was a stickler about not bearing false witness against her neighbor. "And I honestly don't see how we can be wrong. Do you?"

CHAPTER 4

Hazel hauled herself out of the rocker and began fiddling with her coat buttons. "By the way, you haven't said much about this Frankland chap. What's he like?"

"On the tall and burly side. Thirtyish, I should think. I'm never any good at ages."

"Nice-looking?"

"Not bad. He must have a first-rate dentist." Dittany could have been charitable enough to say something agreeable about his smile instead, but she knew what Hazel was driving at: namely that a single young woman with a big house to keep up must automatically view every new man who came along as potential husband material and was he or wasn't he?

"I'll bet you a nickel that's Minerva Oakes's new boarder," Hazel mused. "She was saying at the club that she has a perfectly darling fellow staying there now."

"I know it is because Mrs. MacVicar said so, and all Minerva's boarders are perfect darlings till proven otherwise. Her last perfect darling stole her autographed photo of John Diefenbaker, don't ask me why."

"Probably because it wasn't a picture of Pierre Trudeau instead," sniffed Hazel, a Tory to the bone. "Are you sure Frankland wasn't simply digging in the wrong place?"

"Of course I'm sure. He had a plot plan with Hunneker Land Grant printed right on it and a bunch of dots in red ink marking the places where he was supposed to do his tests. And furthermore, any woman who can even think of Pierre Trudeau without getting goose bumps—"

"If you'd lived with Roger Munson for twenty-three years the only thing that would give you goose bumps would be having to go to the bathroom in the night and not being able to find your bathrobe. How did we get started on politics, anyway? What I want to know is where that map came from. John Architrave never drew a plan in his life. He'd just wander around till his bunions began to twitch and then tell his men to start digging."

"Hazel, you're right! I wondered about that, too. As a guess, I'd say the plan came from the town surveyor's office and the dots were added by somebody who wanted it on the record that tests had been duly performed at certain locations. Doesn't that sound like a typically McNasterish stunt to you? Look, Hazel, is there any chance of pumping Margery Streph a little? Can't you happen to drop in with a cutting from your piggyback plant or something, and get her talking?"

"Oh, I'd have no trouble getting Margery talking." Hazel permitted herself a ladylike snicker. "The problem is, I'd have to wait till she gets back from Calgary. Jim was going there on business, so she went along. That's why we had them to dinner between trips, as a sort of hail-and-farewell party."

"Oh, rats! Then I'll have to think of something else."

"Do. What I've got to think about is what sort of meal I can throw together in three minutes flat." Hazel made for the door. "Thanks for the sherry, Dittany. After I've fed Roger and got him into a good mood, I'll try to joggle his memory and see if he has any idea what Jim Streph was getting at."

Dittany refrained from smiling. Roger did something extremely technical with computers for a large engineering firm over near Scottsbeck. She couldn't imagine his ever having an idea that wasn't too complex for any layman to understand. By the time he'd worked out a viable program and run it through the electronic jungle, the Enchanted Mountain could be one solid mass of blacktop and neon. Why hadn't Hazel had presence of mind enough to marry a member of the town council instead of a walking transistor circuit?

She ate the few sweet meal biscuits that were left on the plate, carried the tray with the used wineglasses back to the kitchen, wondered about supper and decided she wasn't quite ready after all those biscuits, then from force of habit wandered into her workroom and sat down at the typewriter. Since her appetite was temporarily spoiled anyway, she might as well get on with Arethusa's inevitable dueling scene.

Sir Percy tensed the muscles of his finely molded jaw. He was about to pink that rotter Baron Blackavise smack in the right radial extensor and get blood all over his ruffles. Instead, Dittany was astonished to find herself rattling out a scene in which one Andrew McNaster got run plunk through the snuffbox with lethal effect. Maybe she'd better get some solid food inside her, at that.

She fried up a panful of chicken livers with lots of garlic—Gram had always grown it around the roses to keep the bugs away—made herself a green salad, toasted a chunk of her homemade bread, and turned on the television because it was so dismal eating alone.

But the bombings, earthquakes, airplane crashes and other minor diversions of the outside world held little interest in comparison to what was happening here in Lobelia Falls, and when the macho type in the plaid sports jacket began reeling off the hockey scores, she got up and shut off the set. It was almost dark now. Without the light from the picture tube, she could hardly see her plate. The Enchanted Mountain was still plainly visible, though, through the big south-facing kitchen window.

They'd always sat here at mealtimes when there wasn't company, around the golden oak table that had had all its varnish scrubbed off ages ago, with the black iron cookstove warm at their backs in winter as it was warming Dittany now. First there'd been Gram and Gramp and Daddy and Mum and herself in a high chair. Then there'd been Gramp and Daddy and Mum and herself sitting on the telephone book, then there'd been Gramp and Mum and herself big enough to reach her plate without being boosted, then Mum and herself and now there was only herself, sitting where she'd always sat.

And always the mountain had been there. It wasn't so far away, actually. Not so far you couldn't wheel your doll carriage to where the pussytoes grew and still be within sound of your mother's voice calling you to supper. Not too far to watch for Daddy's car turning into Applewood Avenue and run like the dickens so you'd be there when he shut off the motor and called out, "Where's my big girl with a bear hug for her dad?" How would it feel to be sitting here and looking over there and find one's self staring at a brand-new split-level house with a fake fieldstone front and pea-green aluminum sides?

For a moment Dittany lost all interest in her food. Then she began to eat almost angrily. It wasn't going to happen, that was all. She wouldn't let it. She was chasing the last fragment of chicken liver around her plate in a determined and relentless manner when the telephone rang.

That would be Arethusa Monk, no doubt, wanting to know how Sir Percy was getting on. Arethusa took a possessively maternal interest in her brain children, nitwits though they were. Still chewing, Dittany picked up the receiver and managed a mangled "Hello."

No, it was not Arethusa. The novelist had a voice that rang, as Harry Leon Wilson might have described it, like a brazen gong. This was more like a hoarse whisper. At first Dittany assumed it was some youngster playing the same sort of lame-brained trick with the telephone that she and her nasty little friends had played back in their grammar school days. Then she realized she was connected with Mrs. Poppy, the lady who came and did housework once a week provided something more pressing didn't intervene. Mrs. Poppy's excuses for begging off were usually interesting, with that air of fresh spontaneity created by the speaker's making them up as she went along. This one, however, sounded legitimate and dull.

"Miss Henbit," she croaked, "I've had this awful cold since Saturday and now I'm losing my voice. I'm sure I'll be too sick to come tomorrow and I thought I'd better let you know while I can still talk."

That was an interesting change. Mrs. Poppy's customary approach was to wait until about five minutes after she was due to arrive, then deliver her fairy tale in tones of well-feigned panic. She really must be ill.

"What a shame," said Dittany as she had said so often before, but meaning it this time. "You do sound perfectly awful. Are you staying in bed and keeping warm?"

Mrs. Poppy said she was trying to but Miss Henbit knew how it was with a husband and three kids to feed. Miss Henbit didn't know how it was, never having been in that position herself, but she said she could imagine and did Mrs. Poppy think she might be able to make it later in the week?

"I'll have to wait and see how I feel," Mrs. Poppy gargled. "You know me, if there's one thing I hate it's saying I'll come and then having to let a person down. As it is, I'm going to renege on Mrs. Duckes and I feel awful about that. I said I'd fill in for her tonight because she's down with her leg again and you know how she depends on the money."

Dittany didn't know that, either. She had a vague idea who Mrs. Duckes was, but the details of that lady's pecuniary situation were to her as a riddle wrapped in an enigma. However, she obligingly asked, "What were you supposed to do for Mrs. Duckes?" since Mrs. Poppy was always gratified when she showed an interest and she was, in spite of everything, fond of Mrs. Poppy.

"Oh, didn't I tell you?" Her off-and-on employee, sick as she was, appeared to perk up at this chance to impart some news. "Mrs. Duckes got a job working for McNaster Construction. She's supposed to go in every night after they close up, see, and empty the wastebaskets and tidy around and wash out the teacups and that. She says it's a scandal how many half-empty cups of tea they leave sitting around. Not that McNaster's hurting for the money to buy it, I daresay. No flies on him, they say, though Mrs. Duckes says he's not the easiest person in the world to work for, which I know you won't repeat because you know how things get back to people and there she'd be. He's going to be hopping mad tomorrow when he goes in and finds she hasn't been. I just hope he doesn't fire her on account of me. I'd feel awful."

"I'm sure you would."

Dittany made the response automatically but even as she spoke a great light was dawning. "You know, Mrs. Poppy, I have nothing special to do this evening. I could go over there and pinch-hit for you."

"You? Oh, Miss Henbit, that wouldn't be right."

"Why not? I know I'm not the world's prize housekeeper, but at least I could empty the wastebaskets and wash the teacups so they'd know somebody had been around."

"Well, my gosh," croaked Mrs. Poppy, "I never would have—I hope you don't think I was—it would certainly be a Godsend for Mrs. Duckes, but—you don't honestly mean it, do you?"

"Certainly I mean it. Think of all the favors you've done for me." Dittany couldn't think of any herself offhand, but she knew it was the sort of argument Mrs. Poppy would fall for.

Now that she'd committed herself, she was scared but exhilarated. No doubt Mrs. Poppy thought she was slightly crazy, but she'd be crazier still to miss the chance of poking around McNaster's inner sanctum. To be sure, she hadn't the faintest idea what to look for, but the chances were she'd recognize it if she saw it, assuming there was anything to see. Having long been aware that the best way to wring a decision from Mrs. Poppy was to take it for granted the decision had already been made, she said crisply, "What time am I supposed to show up?"

"About seven or quarter past is when Mrs. Duckes generally goes over. She gets supper on the table, eh, then she leaves the dishes for Jenny to do. That's her oldest and of course Jenny's like the rest of them at that age but it doesn't hurt her to pitch in and show a little sense of responsibility as I was saying to—"

"Right. How do I get in?"

"I've put the keys in the sugar bowl right here on the mantelpiece. Mrs. Duckes sent Jenny over with them this morning after I said I'd do it on her way to school but my cold's kept getting worse and worse and now I'm so choked up—"

"Yes, you mustn't say another word. I'll be there to pick them up as soon as I can get ready."

Dittany hung up before Mrs. Poppy could think of any more reasons why she couldn't talk, and whizzed into action. Too bad she didn't have a Jenny of her own to stick with the dishes, but they could wait. The important thing now was to think up a disguise.

Having typed so many of Arethusa's effusions, Dittany had a natural inclination toward cloaks and daggers. Furthermore, if anyone she knew happened to catch her emptying Andy McNasty's wastebaskets, it wouldn't be good publicity for the Henbit Secretarial Service. And besides, there had been that black form sprawled on the mountain with the arrow through its back and maybe it wasn't an accident, and maybe Andrew McNaster was a better shot than he let on to be.

CHAPTER 5

The phone rang several times while Dittany was upstairs changing. She let it ring. Curiosity about John Architrave's death would be building and word must have got round that Dittany Henbit had been among those present when the body was discovered. Now that their families were fed and the tables cleared, her friends wanted the details. They'd have to wait. She had more urgent business at hand.

Luckily the former Mrs. Henbit was a woman of adventurous tastes when she got turned loose in a store, and luckily Mum had left many of her more insane purchases behind when she'd flown off into the wild blue yonder with Bert. Dittany ran her mind over the inventory.

There was that lovely red wig, for one thing. At any rate the wig had been lovely till Mum had worn it in her dramatic triumph as the Madwoman of Chaillot with the Traveling Thespians, who in fact never traveled any farther than the high school auditorium. Since then it had been lent to sundry neighborhood children for dressing up at Halloween and had gone overboard into the apple-bobbing tub on several occasions. The wig should do nicely.

Plenty of makeup was available in all shades and varieties. Dittany sat down at her mother's dressing table—she'd kept the room pretty much as Mum had left it since she never knew when Bert's business would bring the pair of them back here—and set to work.

First she laid on a foundation that was labeled Maiden's Blush but came out looking more like Hectic Flush. Over this bright pink base she dotted a luxuriant crop of freckles, for which she'd always yearned as a child. Then, selecting a Sultry Sable eyebrow pencil, she obscured her own pleasantly arched brows with a ferocious black pair that came up to points in their middles and swooped down toward her nose. She added Pixie Purple, Tantalizing Tan, and Frosted Banana eyeshadow in alternating bands and veiled her blue-green eyes with a screen of inch-long false lashes set on slightly askew because time was running short. By this stage it was a fairly safe bet her own mother wouldn't have known her unless of course Mum happened to recognize the wig.

Encouraged with her progress thus far, Dittany shed the clothes she had on, pulled on an old sweatshirt of Gramp's to make her look fatter and covered that with an awning-striped tent dress that had been one of her mother's biggest mistakes ever. Maroon knee socks and holey old sneakers through which the socks peeped here and there completed the ensemble.

If that didn't do it, nothing would. Dittany put on a long hooded raincoat to hide the costume, hoped Mrs. Poppy would be too preoccupied with her own woes to notice what she'd done to her face, and scrambled for her car keys. Five minutes later Old Faithful, the 1966 Plymouth that had served the Henbit family through thick and thin, snow and sleet, trips to the dump and Girl Guides getting carsick on the seats, pulled up in front of the Poppy home.

It was perhaps fortunate for Mrs. Poppy's fragile state of health that Dittany didn't have to confront her in person. A teen-aged girl dressed not unlike Dittany herself explained that Ma felt so awful she'd gone to bed with a couple of aspirins, and handed over the McNaster office keys along with a few sketchy and no doubt misleading instructions.

Dittany said thanks and sped off into the darkness before this budding Poppy could get too close a look at her.

She knew all too well where to go. The McNaster Construction Company offices, in all their chrome and stucco hideousness, sat out beside the main highway to Scottsbeck on land that had been cleared, landscaped, and given a blacktopped parking lot before the town council suddenly decided the site was, after all, unsuitable for the proposed high school annex. They'd then sold the lot to the ubiquitous Andrew at a scandalous figure on the pretext that his bid, though far too low, was the only one received by their appointed deadline when everyone knew perfectly well that several other firms would have bid more if they'd known about the deadline before it had already passed.

As Dittany pulled into the serendipitous parking lot, she was rather disconcerted to see several other cars including Andy McNasty's own brand-new twenty-thousand-dollar gas guzzler still there. Either they were holding some sort of after-hours meeting or else everybody was working overtime. That didn't bode well for her chances of doing any effective snooping. She might have known this harebrained scheme would come to nothing. Well, she'd got herself into it so there wasn't much she could do now but go through the motions and clear out before her eyelashes fell off.

Mrs. Poppy's daughter had mentioned something about a side door from the parking lot. Dittany managed to locate it and found it open. The girl hadn't mentioned there'd be a tough-looking watchman lurking just inside. Luckily he was nobody Dittany recognized but he scared her half to death anyway.

True to his trust, the watchman offered challenge the moment Dittany set sneaker inside the door. She explained in a hoarse voice that was partly assumed and partly stark terror that she was pinch-hitting for Mrs. Duckes, who was down with her leg again, and where did they keep the brooms and stuff because the kid that gave her the keys didn't know nothing and she didn't want to bother Mrs. Duckes because she was in bed with a couple of aspirins—Dittany saw no point in dragging Mrs. Poppy into her monologue—and where was she supposed to dump the wastebaskets and was it okay if she didn't vacuum but just dusted around and straightened up because she was only doing it as a favor, not that she minded because Mrs. Duckes would do the same for her, and where the heck was that mop closet because how could you expect a person to get anything done if nobody showed her where the stuff was?

By then Dittany was genuinely hoarse and the watchman looking totally bored as she'd hoped he would. With any luck, he'd steer well clear of her from now on. He did condescend to lead her to the mop closet, roll out a large canvas hamper for the trash, and tell her to leave it down here by the door and he'd attend to it later. Dittany was warming up for an elaborate complaint about the mop bucket when the watchman fled out of earshot and the first small victory was hers.

She selected a tasteful assortment of mops and dusters, loaded them into the hamper, and dragged her collection to what she gathered must be the reception area, a typically McNasterish assemblage of imitation wood paneling, monstrous plastic philodendrons in styrofoam pots, vivid green wall-to-wall carpeting, and a truly revolting abstract painting that looked like an explosion in a pickle factory hanging behind a salmon-pink metal desk that held a green phone, a white phone, a red phone, a box of pale mauve tissues, and a digital clock with a picture of Spider Man on the dial. There she picked up one of the dusters and began flapping it around with an air of great industry in case the watchman hadn't really gone.

She did manage to sneak a look at the contents of the wastebasket as she dumped it into the hamper, but learned only that the receptionist chewed sugarless gum, drank diet cola, and needed a new bottle of Sexy Siren nail polish, or so she deduced from the empty one that showed up in the trash. It must have been a dull day at the front office.

Trailing the tools of her adopted trade, Dittany worked her way through the ill-planned one-story building. McNaster employed more desk workers than she'd realized, but aside from the facts that some of them smoked too much and they were one and all incapable of hitting a wastebasket at close range with a wad of paper, she learned nothing of interest. Even when she became emboldened to search their desk drawers she found only what people's desks might logically be expected to contain: pictures of wives and babies, tangles of rubber bands and paper clips, half-eaten candy bars, cough drops, empty aspirin bottles, mechanical pencils with no lead in them, felt-tipped pens that had run dry, ballpoints that had probably never worked at all, stationery, graph paper, blueprints, contract forms, and in one drawer a cache of the sort of magazines that led her to suspect this particular employee didn't keep his mind fully occupied with the construction business.

By now her canvas hamper was almost full, her mop trailing an impressive agglomeration of fuzz, her dusters thoroughly begrimed and her face no doubt the same. She was tired, fed up, and also puzzled. There were all those cars in the parking lot, but so far she hadn't run into one living person except the watchman. The logical inference was that they must all be together somewhere, but where? Not in the conference room. She'd already cleaned that, or tried to. It appeared to be used mainly as a catchall for oddments like billheads, lumber, plastic moldings, the handles for about three hundred kitchen cabinets, half a sundial, two lobster buoys, the remains of a salami sandwich, somebody's golf umbrella, and a plastic flamingo on a long green rod that was presumably meant to be planted in the lawn of somebody who didn't know any better.

There was one closed door at the far end of the corridor. Unless they were all down cellar inspecting the boiler, they must be behind that. So what should she do? Tiptoe past? Knock boldly? Or simply barge in and start mopping?

Why not knock and then barge? That was what she was ostensibly here for, wasn't it? Clutching her mop as a Roman legionary might have elevated his eagle, Dittany approached the fateful orifice. Somehow or other her feet showed a tendency to drag, though certainly not from the weight of her sneakers as there wasn't all that much left of them. Her knuckles also showed a surprising reluctance to rise to the occasion.

In plain fact, now that the moment of truth, if such a commodity existed at McNaster Construction, was at hand, Dittany was scared stiff. She stood there like Lot's wife after that regrettable incident at Sodom, gritting her teeth and cursing herself inwardly for a poltroon, a caitiff knave, and a scurvy varlet. As she lingered, however, she gradually became aware that the door, like everything else McNaster built, was of shoddy quality and poorly hung. By straining her ears only a little, she could hear pretty much everything of the discussion that was taking place inside the room.

"What do you think I'm paying you for?" somebody was demanding angrily.

"Now, Andy," somebody else replied in a tone that could best be described as unctuous, "we all know what you pay me for, and I'm sure everybody here would agree that I've always come through for you. But what you want now is simply too hot for me to handle. I could wind up being run out of Scottsbeck and disbarred for life. And if I was put in a position where I faced criminal prosecution, I'm sure you realize it wouldn't be in my best interest to keep quiet. These people here in Lobelia Falls can't possibly be quite such idiots as you seem to think they are."

"But you said yourself the trust could be broken," McNaster argued. "Look, Charlie, I want that land and I mean to have it. You're making a big song and dance out of a simple little deal. All you have to do is draw up the papers. Then as soon as Sam here gets elected to the Development Commission, he strong-arms those other dodoes into passing an emergency ordinance and it's in the bag."

"And suppose for the sake of argument Sam doesn't get elected? Then I'd be left holding that bag you so casually mention."

"How the hell can Sam not get elected? Nobody's running against him, and it's too late now to file nomination papers. The election's next Tuesday, for the cat's sake! Sam's a shoo-in. Right, Sam?"

"Right," said a voice Dittany knew all too well and would never have dreamed of hearing in these surroundings. "I'm in like Flynn. The only way anybody could vote against me now would be on a write-in ballot, and who's going to bother? You know who turns out for these local elections, about six old diehards and the candidate's relatives. Anyway, I'm a popular man. Everybody knows who's the public-spirited citizen who kicks in the eggnog for the Old Folks' Christmas Party and the keg of beer for the Policemen's Picnic and all those other benevolent gestures."

"Which he takes off his income tax as charitable deductions," mocked a voice Dittany couldn't identify.

Her fear had turned to rage. The public-spirited citizen was Sam Wallaby, proprietor of Lobelia Falls's one and only liquor store. Sam had even donated the sauterne and Seven-Up for the mock champagne punch at the Grub-and-Stakers' Spring Flower Festival year before last and she herself, as then Corresponding Secretary, had been delegated to write him a nice little thank-you note. She'd even spent two dollars of her own money for a box of pretty flowered stationery to write it on. To think she'd been an unwitting tool of his perfidy!

"See, Charlie," McNaster went on in a coaxing tone, "you don't have a thing to worry about. This deal will go smooth as a kitten's wrist. Before anybody knows what's happening, I'll have me a swell big house right smack-dab on top of that Enchanted Mountain. And you guys can live around the edges."

"Catch me living in any house you'd build," chortled the unidentified voice.

Charlie was not convinced. "I don't care, Andy. I'm not going to risk having my name linked with the kind of mud you're bound to stir up. And I particularly don't like the business of old Architrave's getting shot with a black arrow up there this morning. If that's the way you're going to play it—"

"Hey, wait a minute!" yelped McNaster. "You don't think I had anything to do with that?"

"Andy, as a lawyer I know better than to make any direct accusation. I'm simply saying it happened at a strangely opportune time. Architrave might have been stupid, but I don't recall ever having heard he was dishonest, beyond reasonable limits. You might have got him to rush those leaching tests through, but I doubt if you could have persuaded him to falsify the results."

"Charlie, you're crazy. It was a hunter from the States. Everybody knows that."

"I don't know it, do I?"

"Look, I was right here in my office all day. Anyway, I'm not the world's best shot, as any of these boys here can tell you. Hell, I don't mind being kidded about it, but if you think I—"

"I'm only going by the evidence, Andy. I have no doubt that you have an alibi tighter than a drum. But you do have a fairly large staff, Andy. And among them may be some good shots and some talented liars. Mind you, I'm not making any accusations. I'm just stating what might be termed an academic hypothesis. And you needn't start yelling because you wouldn't dare fire me and we both know it."

"The hell I wouldn't! If you think—"

"That's just it, Andy. I do think. And it will pay you to think. Regardless of how Architrave was killed, the fact remains that his death is going to focus attention on this Hunneker Land Grant. People are already asking questions about why he had that new chap up there doing perk tests. Who was that woman from the Conservation Committee?"

McNaster said an extremely bad word. "I wish I knew. What the hell, this town doesn't even have a Conservation Committee. Some old bag with a bee in her bonnet about the pretty pussy willows, maybe. For all I know, she was the one who plugged him."

"Well, you'd better find out what she was up to and how much she knows or guesses if you know what's good for you. Look, Andy, I'm backing out of this mess as far as I can get. If you want to take the risk of going ahead with your plan, I can put you in touch with a very capable colleague of mine who happens to be on loan, as you might say, from one of the eastern provinces, on account of a little problem he ran into there. He won't mind handling your legal matter because he's planning to immigrate to Tasmania in the near future anyway. You can then explain to anybody who's interested that you went to all the extra expense and bother of calling in an expert from out of town in order to be sure of getting an opinion that would be totally free of any local bias or possible self-interest."

Everybody thought that was pretty hilarious. Hearing them in there laughing their heads off made Dittany so furious she could think of nothing but getting in there to see who they were. She tried the knob, found the door locked, but managed to fit in one of the keys Mrs. Poppy had given her. As she turned the latch, she heard somebody yelp, "What the hell?" and make a rush for the door. Before she could get it open more than a crack, it was held fast from inside and one of Andrew McNaster's beady little eyes glared through the slit.

"What do you want? Haven't I told you—"

"Want me to clean in there?" Dittany interrupted in that hoarse, toneless voice she'd practiced on the night watchman.

"No," he roared. "Haven't I told you never to bother me when I'm in conference? Who the hell are you, anyway? Where's the woman who usually comes?"

Dittany had been doing bit parts with the Traveling Thespians since she was five and, since she always forgot her lines, she'd developed a ready talent for improvisation. "You'll have to speak up, mister. My hearin' aid's in for repairs. Do I clean in there or don't I? See, Mrs. Duckes's bad leg kicked up on 'er again so I said I'd help out but she never told me if I was s'posed to—"

"Just go away," yelled McNaster at the top of his lungs. He opened the door just far enough to thrust a bill into her hand, then slammed it in her face.

Dittany went to put away her mops and dusters. As she did so, she looked at the money McNaster had given her. It was a twenty. How nice. He didn't know it, but he'd just made the first donation to Sam Wallaby's rival's campaign fund. Getting Sam defeated was going to take some doing, though, since they had less than a week to campaign in. And there was the further problem of whom she could get to run.

CHAPTER 6

This was no time to worry about a candidate. She'd better get out of the parking lot before the meeting broke up and one of that skulduggerous crew recognized her car. Sam Wallaby would, for sure. He'd lugged enough imperial quarts of Seagram's out to it while Gramp was alive, not that Gramp Henbit had been any great drinker, but how else could an old man keep his creaking joints oiled? Dittany herself had retained the habit of keeping a little anti-freeze on hand for emergencies, though she assuredly wouldn't be buying any more from Sam Wallaby.

She did wish Andy McNasty had opened that office door wide enough for her to see who else was inside. On the other hand she was rather glad he hadn't. Charlie, that shyster lawyer from Scottsbeck, had made it all too clear, in spite of his legalistic evasions, what he thought about Mr. Architrave's strange and sudden demise. Dittany admitted to herself that she couldn't swallow any theory about a phantom hunter. Even Hazel Munson, who bent over backward never to think ill of anyone, had come right out and suggested murder. They'd guessed at a motive; now Dittany knew it was more than a guess. She stomped on Old Faithful's accelerator and headed straight for the neat red brick house with the green trim at the corner of Hickory and Vine.

The Munsons would have finished supper well before this. They lived by a schedule programmed to the minute by Roger though not always adhered to by Hazel and the younger Munsons, who ranged from almost grown up to turbulent ten. This was Roger's Be Pals with Your Kids night, so he and they would be off to the skating rink, leaving Hazel to Enjoyment of Unin-

terrupted Leisure, which for her was apt to mean catching up on
the mending or baking a fancy dessert. Tonight her leisure was
going to be interrupted in a way Roger would never have
dreamed of programming.

Dittany brought Old Faithful to a screaming halt two inches
from the doorstep, rushed up, and pounded like mad on the brass
knocker. Hazel appeared promptly, inched the door open on the
chain, and said suspiciously, "Yes?"

"Hazel," snapped Dittany, "quit playing games and let me in."

"Good heavens, Dittany, is that you?" Hazel released the
chain. "What on God's green earth have you done to yourself?
Here, give me that." She picked up the raincoat Dittany dropped
and hung it in the closet. As Roger always said, Neatness was
Efficiency. "Now what's this all about?"

"Hazel, listen. You know Mrs. Poppy?"

"Of course I know Mrs. Poppy. She's that woman who's supposed to come and clean for you but never does."

"She does sometimes," said Dittany defensively. "Anyway,
Mrs. Poppy has a friend, Mrs. Duckes, who does the office at
McNaster's every evening after work. I mean after he and his
staff—oh, you know what I mean. Anyway, this Mrs. Duckes
has a bad leg—I don't know which or why so don't bother to ask
—and Mrs. Poppy was going to fill in for her but she caught a
bad cold. She called me up while I was having my supper to tell
me she couldn't come tomorrow because she was too sick and
then she went croaking on about how she'd promised to do the
offices for Mrs. Duckes and how awful she felt about letting her
down."

"Were you planning to get to the point any time in the fore-
seeable future?"

"But that is the point, Hazel. I said I'd go to McNaster's in her
place, and I did."

"Dittany, you didn't!"

"What's the sense in saying I didn't when I just got through
telling you I did?"

"The exclamation was purely rhetorical. I only meant, my
gosh, how did you ever have the nerve?"

"Frankly, I'm not sure," Dittany admitted. "You wouldn't believe how scary it can be opening a strange broom closet."

Hazel took her guest gently by the arm and led her to Roger's pet reclining chair. "Here, sit down and put your feet up, eh? I'm going to make us a pot of hot tea. You must be in shock. It won't take a second."

Dittany was glad to obey. All of a sudden, like Mrs. Duckes, she was having trouble with her legs. She lay back and shut her eyes until Hazel came back with a tea tray on which, to Dittany's unalloyed joy, was a slab of her superb carrot-walnut-allspice cake with orange coconut frosting.

"Eat this with your tea. The sweet will be good for you."

Dittany needed no coaxing. Disregarding the fact that she'd been carefully taught never to talk with her mouth full, she wolfed her cake and told her story at the same time.

"McNaster was having a meeting with some men in his private office. The door was locked, but I listened outside. And I heard him having an argument about the Enchanted Mountain with some crooked lawyer whom he wanted to help him get hold of the land."

"You didn't! I'm sorry. You did. Dittany, why?"

"Because he wants to build himself a big house right smack-dab on top. Those were his own words, Hazel, right smack-dab on top. And he talked about building some more houses around the sides and that must be what he's got Jim Streph working on the plans for. And that's why that Frankland man was doing the perk tests, and why Mr. Architrave got murdered just as we thought."

"Dittany, he—I mean, are you sure?"

"Well, this lawyer as much as accused McNaster of having one of his henchmen bump Mr. Architrave off because he was too honest to fake the results of the tests even if he was dumb enough to do them in the first place, which is true enough."

"Yes, it is," said Hazel slowly. "And he was pigheaded enough to stick to his guns no matter what. I don't see myself how that land could be buildable unless they ran sewer pipes because it's all ledge under the leaf mold. That must be why McNaster wanted the tests done before the frost was out, so he could pretend they were hitting frozen ground instead of rock. He's got away with so many other things, I suppose he'd be cocky enough to think even a fool stunt like that would work."

"Only he didn't count on having a new man with a few brains in his head join the department just at the wrong time," Dittany added. "Frankland did say he'd protested to Mr. Architrave about the ground being too hard to give a proper reading. Maybe that finally penetrated the old man's skull and he got to wondering about it himself and that's why he went up there today and that's why McNaster had him killed. And, Hazel, I think they're putting out a contract on me."

"A what?"

"I think that's what they call it." Dittany wasn't sure, having watched only one television crime show in her life and found it dull stuff in comparison to any average day's doings around Lobelia Falls. "Anyway, the lawyer—McNaster called him Charlie and I got the impression that he's from Scottsbeck—said Andy had better find out who that woman from the Conservation Committee was if he knew what was good for him, and what was good for him would automatically have to be bad for me, wouldn't it?"

"Maybe you'd better put that wig back on before you leave," Hazel replied in a worried tone. "How did they know you were from the Conservation Committee without knowing your name too?"

"I mentioned the committee when I was yelling at that Frankland man to get off the Spotted Pipsissewa, and I didn't tell him who I was until after that arrow had been fired. So the man who shot Mr. Architrave must have been right there on the other side of the ridge where he could hear me but not see me, and ran away as soon as he'd loosed his second arrow. Or she did," Dittany added, thinking of her meager gleanings from the receptionist's wastebasket. "The woman in the front office didn't seem to have done much of anything today. Maybe she was busy elsewhere. I wonder who she is and how heavy a bow she pulls."

"That's a thought, Dittany. She wouldn't be anybody local.

You know McNaster can't get anybody from Lobelia Falls to work for him because we all hate his guts. I must say I can't imagine why Jim Streph does, though he's so wrapped up in his art that he'd design new hinges for the doors of Hell if the Devil asked him to, and never think twice about where the money was coming from. But surely McNaster didn't admit he'd put somebody up to killing old John?"

"Naturally not. He blustered around and claimed he didn't know a thing about it, but what would you expect? Anyway, this Charlie kept insisting McNaster had better drop the idea of stealing the land. Even if he wasn't guilty he'd get into trouble because Mr. Architrave's death would focus public attention on the Enchanted Mountain. But McNaster said he wouldn't because it's all sewed up."

"How, for goodness' sake? Not that goodness has anything to do with it, obviously."

"You sound like Mae West. That's the most fantastic part of all, Hazel. You know Sam Wallaby is running for Development Commission, eh?"

"Is he? I'm afraid I hadn't paid much attention."

"Then you darn well should because he was right there in that office with the rest of them."

"Sam Wallaby from the liquor store? That's impossible. He's always so nice about donating—"

"The eggnog for the Old Folks' Christmas Party. I know. He was laughing his head off about how nobody could run against him because everybody thinks he's such a fine, public-spirited citizen. And when I think of the two bucks I wasted on that fancy stationery so I could write him a nice thank-you note for the sauterne and Seven-Up we had at the flower show, I could spit!"

Hazel sat back and shook her head. "I simply cannot believe it."

"Then you just sit back and fold your hands and see what's going to happen as soon as they get him safely planted on the Development Commission. This Charlie's going to get some gangster lawyer he knows who's on the lam—I believe it's the lam—anyway he's going to do the paper work and escape to Tasmania and bang goes the Heart-leaved Twayblade."

"Oh, Dittany!" At last Hazel was forced to grasp the hideous reality of the situation. "They could, you know. They did it before when they passed that emergency ordinance to get around the need for holding public hearings and took over that old chicken farm that was supposed to be the high school annex when any idiot could see it was the worst possible place for a school, and when they got it all graded and blacktopped they went through that farce about the bids and now—"

"And now that's where McNaster's sitting with his cronies cooking up another dirty deal," Dittany finished for her. "I've got a good notion to march straight over to Sergeant MacVicar and tell him what I heard."

"I'm not so sure about that," Hazel cautioned. "Maybe you don't remember, but Mrs. MacVicar happens to be Andy McNasty's mother's own cousin, though naturally she doesn't care to have it generally mentioned. And blood's thicker than water when all's said and done, and it's only your word against his and if he's got Sam Wallaby on his side—Dittany, what are we going to do?"

"Well, I know one thing we can do because Sam Wallaby himself told me. Not on purpose, naturally, but he was gassing on to this Charlie the lawyer about how he's an absolute certain shoo-in because nobody filed nomination papers against him and it's too late now. And he said the only way anybody could possibly defeat him would be through a write-in campaign, which isn't going to happen because he's such a sterling character and nobody bothers to vote in town elections anyway. So we're going to put up a write-in candidate and we're going to get out that vote and we're going to lick the pants off that smarmy walrus and spike McNaster's guns. Look!" She pulled out the twenty-dollar bill. "Andy McNasty gave me this."

"Whatever for?"

"To get rid of me. After I'd heard all this stuff I thought I'd better get a look at who was with him, so I unlocked the door but he came rushing over and held it so I couldn't see inside. All I could see was his right eye."

"That would have been more than enough for me," said Hazel fervently. "Whatever did you do then?"

"Pretended I was deaf as a post and couldn't hear him yelling at me to go away because needless to say I didn't want him to know I'd been eavesdropping all that time. I started giving him a rigmarole about Mrs. Duckes's sore leg and my hearing aid's being broken and was I supposed to clean in there or wasn't I, and he shoved this money in my hand and slammed the door in my face. Would you call that the act of an honest man?"

"I certainly can't imagine Roger doing such a thing. Naturally he'd know the customary rates for maintenance personnel—"

"Which, whatever they may be, aren't enough. Hazel, how would you feel about running for Development Commission?"

"Who, me? Dittany, I couldn't possibly. I almost fainted dead away when I had to get up at the last annual meeting and read the report of the club's Ways and Means Committee. Why don't you run yourself?"

"Because I'm basically unconvincing. People tend not to take me seriously. I can't think why."

One of Dittany's false eyelashes had vanished completely, the other was hanging at a rakish angle from her left eyebrow. Her face was an interesting mélange of Maiden's Blush, Pixie Purple, Tantalizing Tan, Frosted Banana, Sultry Sable, and McNaster grime. Gramp Henbit's sweatshirt caused her mother's awning-striped tent to bulge in odd places. Her fine hair was matted into ducktails from being crammed under the wig, her maroon socks rucked down around her well-ventilated sneakers. Oblivious of these facts, she sat licking orange coconut icing off her cake fork. Hazel forbore to comment.

"Besides," Dittany added, laying down the now totally de-iced fork with obvious regret, "I'm a marked woman. The more I go barging around making noises in public, the sooner Andy McNasty's going to identify me as the old bag from the Conservation Committee. I'd have to fly the coop or blow the scene or whatever the correct procedure is in such cases and you'd still be without a candidate. What we need is somebody stately and dignified and poised yet forceful like—"

"Samantha Burberry!" cried Hazel.

"Precisely the name I was about to utter. Come on, eh, let's get cracking."

"You mean right this minute? Dittany, we can't simply pick up our heels and go lippity-lipping over to the Burberrys'."

"Why can't we?"

"Well," floundered Hazel, overcome by shyness and not wishing to admit it, "Joshua will be home."

"So what? He's a registered voter, isn't he? We'll appeal to his sense of civic responsibility and sign him up as a sponsor."

"But he's a college professor!"

"Is there something in the election rules about college professors not being sponsors? Hazel, you're not by any chance weaseling out on me, are you? Think of the Climbing Fumitory. Think of the Hairy Beardtongue. Think of Andy McNasty up on top of the Enchanted Mountain sticking plastic flamingos all over his brand-new Astroturf lawn."

"Dittany, he wouldn't!"

But Hazel knew in her heart of hearts that he would. Sighing, she put on her coat, picked up her house keys, and followed Dittany Henbit out into the night.

CHAPTER 7

"Wouldn't you like to stop at your house before we go on to the Burberrys'?" Hazel suggested gently.

"What for?" asked Dittany.

"Well, for one thing, your eyelashes are molting."

"Oh. I expect I could do with a little titivating, eh?" Dittany picked off a small twig that had somehow worked its way through one of the holes in her right sneaker. "Poor Joshua must get enough sartorial shocks in the course of a day without my adding another. Samantha says he almost cried when he heard a rumor that miniskirts were coming back into fashion. He told her there's nothing in the world so depressing as walking into a class at half past seven on a nasty November morning and finding one's self staring down at a roomful of panty girdles."

"Nobody would believe what teachers go through," Hazel agreed somberly. "I taught two years before I was married, and I'd rather scrub floors any day."

"Speaking of scrubbing floors," Dittany mused, "I expect I ought to get these keys back to Mrs. Poppy. All things considered, it might not be a particularly brilliant idea for McNaster to find out I have them."

"I think it would be an abysmally rotten idea," Hazel concurred. "Is there any hope whatever of persuading Mrs. Poppy to keep quiet about your having gone in her place?"

"I can't imagine Mrs. Poppy's keeping quiet about anything whatsoever. Besides, her family already know. At least her daughter does, the one who came to the door."

"Then you'll have to appeal to their better natures and you'd better do it right away."

"Before I wash my face?"

"No, after. By all means after."

Once they'd ridden the short distance to her own house and she'd got a look at herself in the bathroom mirror, Dittany recognized the wisdom of Hazel's suggestion. She slathered on a large gob of the former Mrs. Henbit's Lady Godiva Take It All Off Makeup Remover, disentangled her eyelid from the remaining lashes, and got her face back to what the late U. S. President Warren G. Harding would have termed normalcy. She changed out of the tent dress and sweatshirt into a trim corduroy outfit as befitted a lady of serious purpose and, at Hazel's prompting, discarded the maroon knee socks and ruined sneakers in favor of neat brown boots.

Then she put her raincoat back on, picked up her handbag containing the fateful bunch of keys, loaded Hazel aboard, and again headed Old Faithful Poppyward. On this occasion it was not the daughter but the man of the house who answered the door. His wife, he informed Miss Henbit with no appearance of pleasure, was upstairs asleep.

"I do hope she'll feel better in the morning," said Dittany, handing over the keys. "When she wakes up, would you mind giving her these and telling her I managed reasonably well, all things considered. Oh, and—er—would you just mention that I'd rather not have her tell anybody who took her place?"

"Why not?" he growled, eyeing the keys suspiciously.

"Well, you see," Dittany floundered, "I'd—er—as soon not have anybody—er—know."

"If you mean your lawful wedded husband why don't you say so?" Mr. Poppy exploded. "What you mean is, if he was to find out you been goin' around to other people's houses instead of stayin' home where a wife belongs an' havin' a hot supper ready for him when he comes off work as was duly stated in the marriage vows when I took Mrs. Poppy for better or worse, which is worse I'm gettin' these days since she took a notion to have a career like Glorious Sternum an' the rest of them Commie pinko women's libbers, he'd be as ticked off as I am and I for one wouldn't blame him!" Mr. Poppy whacked the ringful of keys on the palm of his other hand for emphasis, sustained a minor flesh wound, and glared at Dittany as though it were all her fault.

"Well, no, I didn't mean my husband," Dittany made the mistake of trying to explain. "I don't have one, but I do run a business of my own. If word got round that I'd gone out cleaning, my clients might begin to think—well, you know how it is."

"I know how it is," roared Mr. Poppy, "and I DON'T LIKE HOW IT IS!" He glowered at Dittany a while longer, then asked in a slightly less belligerent tone, "What kind o' business?"

"I'm a secretarial service."

"Blah! I bet my wife makes out better than you do."

"I know she does," Dittany confessed. "I'm one of the people she cleans for."

"Not anymore you ain't. I've had it, see? I'm puttin' my foot down. Goin' out an' inhalin' other people's germs an' gettin' herself laid up when she promised faithful she'd make me a good pot o' pea soup like my mother used to. Ruinin' her health for a bunch of ingrates!"

He started to whack the keys again, thought better of it, and slammed the door in her face instead. Sighing, Dittany went back to the car where Hazel was waiting.

"How did you make out?"

"Don't ask!" Needless to say, Dittany told her anyway. "So I've lost a housekeeper on top of everything else. Honestly, Hazel, I don't know what I'm going to do if Mr. Poppy doesn't simmer down. I can't cope with that big place and earn a living too. I couldn't cope even if I didn't have to work. Housekeeping to me is as a mystery sealed whence no man knoweth the key thereof."

"You're getting to talk like Arethusa Monk."

"Oh yeah? Wait till you hear the kind of language Arethusa uses when she finds out. Mrs. Poppy works for her too."

"Don't borrow trouble, eh? I daresay Mrs. Poppy can straighten out Mr. Poppy once she gets her voice back."

"Anyhow, he didn't have to call me an ingrate," Dittany muttered. "I only hope Joshua doesn't come all over male chauvinist, too, and put his foot down on Samantha."

"How could he?" Hazel pointed out reasonably. "He's half a head shorter than she is, so it would be physically impossible. Anyway, he's probably off in his study pasting together a split atom or whatever it is they do."

As to the duties and occupations of a professor of physics, Hazel might be pardoned for showing a certain vagueness. As to his non-interference, she was right on the button. The stumbling block they encountered was Samantha herself.

"I couldn't," she protested. "I simply couldn't."

"Of course you could," Dittany argued. "You served two terms as president of the Grub-and-Stakers, didn't you? You were over-all coordinator for the Spring Flower Festival, weren't you? Did you or did you not do a brilliant job in both positions?"

"Well, I—"

"You were magnificent and you know it. Do you mean to sit there and try to convince us that being on the Development Commission could possibly be more demanding than running a flower show and still have everybody speaking to everybody else when it was over?"

"Well, probably not, but—"

They argued, they pleaded, they appealed to Samantha's sense of civic duty. They dwelt on the perfidy of McNaster, the peril to the Pipsissewa, the wreckage of their club's chances of ever capturing the coveted Lady Matilda Leonora Macklesfield Triple Tricolor Ribbon with Euphorbia Cluster for Wildflower Conservation should the Enchanted Mountain become a disenchanted development. They urged, they cajoled, they finally wept. And all they got from Samantha Burberry was, "I can't do it. I simply can't!"

At last Dittany lost her temper. "Why the flaming heck can't you?"

"Because I—oh, all right. I might as well come clean. Because this coming Sunday I have to give a golden anniversary luncheon for Joshua's parents and they sent me a list of all the people they wanted me to invite and there were seventy-five on the list and all seventy-five accepted."

"Well, what of it? You had four hundred and sixty-two at the Loyalist Ladies' Luncheon you chaired two years ago in Ottawa, didn't you? And they gave you a standing ovation, didn't they?"

"Four hundred and sixty-three," Samantha corrected automatically. "The speaker brought an unexpected guest. And the ovation was mainly on account of the chicken mousse. This is an entirely different situation."

"How is it different?"

"There all I had to do was make sure of the hall and hire the right caterer. This time I have to hold the thing right here in our own house and Joshua won't let me have anybody cater it. He says his parents would have fits if we went to all that extra expense and it would entirely spoil their day."

"And what about your day?"

"Dittany, you're not a married woman, for which fact I sincerely hope you're duly grateful. You simply don't understand about in-laws. Joshua keeps saying it won't happen again for another fifty years and goes maundering on about buying some paper plates and opening a few cans."

"Good heavens, you can't do that," gasped Hazel, her housewifely soul shocked to the core. "Not for a fiftieth anniversary."

"So I keep telling him. It must be done properly or there's no sense in doing it at all, but how? This was Father and Mother Burberry's house before they skipped off and left us holding the tax bills, you know, and they never wanted me to marry Joshua in the first place. They think I'm flighty and frivolous and short in the intellect."

"You?" cried Dittany. "That's ridiculous!"

"Go tell them that, eh? And when I make a hopeless hash of this party, as I'm absolutely certain to do, they're going to look down their noses and sniff and say they might have known and I'm terrified!" Samantha the poised, Samantha the coolly detached, Samantha the unflappable broke down and sobbed. "Whatever am I going to do?"

"I'll tell you what you're going to do," said Dittany. "You're going to stiffen your upper lip and shove all this balderdash behind you and start running for office. I'll manage your campaign and Hazel will handle your party. Right, Hazel?"

"Right," said Hazel absent-mindedly. She was already pacing off the gracious, high-ceilinged living room. "Seventy-five, you said. Plus the two Burberrys and yourself and Joshua. Anyone else? What about the twins?"

These were Samantha's offspring, twenty-year-olds who could never be accused of shortness in the intellect. Though still enrolled at McGill, they had already begun to make their collective mark in the field of entomology.

"They're in Patagonia studying web-footed beetles," Samantha told her. "They couldn't come all the way back here just for a party. Anyway, Father Burberry says science must be served. So far that's the only thing I know of that will be served. I can't cook for seventy-nine people."

"I can," said Hazel. "Quit nattering, Samantha, and leave this to me. So we'll need twenty bridge tables, eighty folding chairs —are these people too doddering to manage a buffet?"

"Lord, no! They all belong to curling clubs and do yoga exercises."

"Good, then we can set up the food in the dining room. It'll be a cinch. Could you find me a paper and pencil?"

"Yes, I should be able to manage that much." A modicum of Samantha's normal calm amusement was beginning to return.

Supplied with writing materials, Hazel began prowling and muttering, jotting things down, shaking her head over the outsize Biedermeier sofa, nodding approval of the gold velvet draperies and bisque-painted walls, cocking an eyebrow at the carved mantelpiece, pondering earnestly over the Persian rugs on the floor, finally wandering into the dining room to commune with her higher self.

Leaving her to it, Dittany ignored whatever further protest Samantha might have in mind about being thrust into politics at this time of marital crisis and got down to basics.

"You'll have to be at the town dump on Saturday morning to

shake hands when people bring their garbage. That's the crux of any successful campaign. And you must put in an appearance at Candidates' Night on Monday evening in the lower town hall. Can you write your own speech or shall I do it for you?"

"You'll have to," Samantha moaned, another wave of despondency hitting her. "All I can think of is what Mother Burberry's going to say when she finds out."

"What do you care if she finds out or not? They're not moving back to Lobelia Falls, are they?"

"God forbid! No, they're just flying in for the party, then going on to a convention at Dalhousie where Father Burberry's going to speak. Joshua's going, too. How are we ever going to cram all those people in this house?"

"Samantha, will you quit worrying? There's plenty of room."

Dittany hadn't the faintest idea whether there was or not, but she'd long ago learned the efficacy of a strong positive statement at a moment of indecision. Besides, the house was one of those nice old unfunctionally planned ones that had lots of agreeably odd-shaped rooms running into one another, including a gloriously wasteful six-sided foyer that could hold at least three card tables and maybe four in a pinch.

"Okay," she went on before Samantha could start stewing again. "I'll write the speech and reserve a spot for you on the program. Whom do you want on your committee?"

"Zilla Trott would be good. She's a real live wire."

"Great." Dittany grabbed another pencil and wrote, Dump. Speech. Zilla. "Now let's see. We'll need some kind of flier to hand out. I can type it up and get Mr. Gumpert at Ye Village Stationer to run off copies on his speedy instant printer. That shouldn't take him more than five or six hours. Then we'll get the members' kids to ride around on their bikes and stuff the flyers under people's doors."

"Wouldn't a telephone squad be more effective? Five members could call five other members and get each one to call five neighbors—no, it's got to be better organized than that." Samantha, her woes forgotten, snatched Dittany's pencil and started making a list of her own. "We'll need a voting list from town hall, divide it into precincts and then into segments, appoint a precinct captain for each segment, get her to round up her own volunteers—"

"Now you're perking," said Dittany. "Good, then you line up the phone squad first thing in the morning, right? We haven't a minute to waste."

"Just don't call any of this lot," said Hazel, thrusting her own list under Samantha's nose. "They're the best cooks in the club and I'll need them for my Luncheon Committee."

"Yes, Hazel. Now, Dittany, what about posters and publicity? And money? Josh and I won't have a spare nickel by the time we get through shelling out for this idiotic party."

Dittany hauled out McNaster's twenty-dollar bill. "Not to worry, Samantha. See, we've already had one donation and that's from the opposition. Wait till we start putting the arm on the good guys! Come on, Hazel, let's go see if Zilla Trott's still up."

CHAPTER 8

Zilla was up, looking handsome and peppy as always in her long red flannel nightgown topped by an experimentally-knitted sweater in a startling shade of pink. Striding easily in her buckskin earth shoes, she led Dittany and Hazel out to the kitchen where she'd been grinding something in a hand mill, dragged out two tall pine stools for them to sit on, and went on grinding.

While the things that came out of Zilla's kitchen were sometimes peculiar, the kitchen itself was a dream. Old grocers' bins stood full of rice, oats, barley, and other grains. Bunches of dried herbs and festoons of onions and garlic hung from hooks in the oaken beams. On the high-backed iron stove the same old curly-nosed graniteware teakettle Zilla's mother had bought new when she got married was sending up gentle puffs of steam.

"Well, this is a nice surprise," cried Zilla, pushing back a strand of iron-gray hair and reaching for three pottery mugs. "I was just going to put my soybeans to sprout and make myself a cup of camomile tea before bedtime. You'll have some, won't you? It soothes the nerves."

"Then you'd better make plenty," Dittany answered. "Zilla, listen."

Zilla listened, her gray locks bouncing ever more violently and her black eyes snapping red fire as she listened to the unfolding tale of McNaster's perfidious intentions and the mystery surrounding Mr. Architrave's alleged accident. Zilla always claimed to be part Cree and she certainly looked it tonight with a scarlet flush spreading like war paint over her high-bridged nose and sun-browned face. Metaphorically speaking, she was already reaching for her tomahawk by the time Dittany finished her bloodcurdling narrative.

"That's outrageous! Infamous! Downright stinking! I can see somebody plugging an arrow through John Architrave in a fit of pique, because he could be the most exasperating old he-devil that ever trod the face of this earth, but for anybody to go wantonly rooting up the only wild place left where I can still get my sassafras and wintergreen is totally inexcusable and of course we're going to stop it. Count me in with bells on and if you need McNaster shot, too, remember I can pull a bow with any man in town."

"Thanks, Zilla," said Dittany with an uneasy feeling that Mrs. Trott might not be joking and a fervent desire not to know whether she'd happened to run short of sassafras earlier on that same day. "I'm hoping we can manage without any more mayhem."

"Maybe so, but we've got to do a good deal more than just get Samantha elected. We'll have to show this half-witted town that we really do care about the Enchanted Mountain."

"But, Zilla, of course we care," said Hazel, sipping suspiciously at her camomile tea. "Why would we be here talking to you right now if we didn't care?"

"I didn't say talk, I said show," snapped Zilla. All that wheat germ she ate tended to accelerate her mental processes and she could wax testy sometimes with those who were slower on the uptake. "We've got to send a work party up there first thing in the morning to clean out the dead wood, pick up trash, tear down the poison ivy, make paths, put up trail markers—"

"Whoa! Hold your horses," gasped Hazel. "It would take an army half a year to do all that. How could we even make a dent, plus run a successful political campaign and put on a bash for eighty people? We've only got till next Tuesday. Monday, actually, because Tuesday's election day and if we haven't got our licks in before then we might as well forget it."

"Well, don't ask me how, Hazel. I'm just telling you it's got to be done and it's got to be done right. If we don't put up a good show, McNaster and his crowd will go blatting around that we're just trying to obstruct progress and stand in the way of free private enterprise and all that garbage. And you know as well as I that there'd be people around here ready to believe them."

"Yes, I know, Zilla, but if we try to spread ourselves too thin —though Lord knows with a figure like mine—"

"Hazel, listen to me. Suppose we do fail to get Samantha elected? I'm not saying we will, but suppose we do? If we've at least managed to demonstrate that this town is genuinely interested in keeping the Enchanted Mountain as a wildflower preserve and fixing it up so people can enjoy it, then we've still got an arrow or two in our quiver to fight McNaster with, haven't we?"

"Yes, Zilla," sighed Hazel. "You're right as usual. I'm sure I don't know what Roger's going to say."

"Who cares?" Zilla replied with her customary tact and finesse. "Come on, let's go rope in Minerva Oakes. She's the other half of the Landscape Committee."

"You rope her. The Luncheon Committee's flaking out for the night, so you can just kiss Minerva for me and ask if she has any big casserole dishes to spare. Mind dropping me at my house, Dittany?"

"Not at all."

Hazel, after all, had done her noblest already and was probably down on her husband's schedule to brew a rousing noggin of Ovaltine for the returning bowlers. Dittany dropped her as requested, then went on with Zilla, who had added an aged sheepskin jacket of her late husband's to her red nightgown, pink sweater, and earth shoes.

By this time Dittany had become so imbued with a sense of her mission that she'd entirely forgotten about Minerva's new boarder until the man from the Water Department smiled at her from behind the cribbage board and got to his feet, looking taller than ever in the low-ceilinged room.

Minerva was delighted at the unexpected visit, her old-rose-petal face crinkled in smiles and dimples. She was short and plump as her friend Zilla was tall and lanky, and a much better knitter. Her own cardigan, though it did stretch a bit over her grandmotherly bosom, was flawlessly done in a tricky pineapple pattern, of bright yellow worsted. It made her look like a somewhat overfed goldfinch that had somehow swapped its black cap for a white one.

"Now this is what I call neighborly. Come in. Haul up an' set, as Aunt Ruby used to say. Here, Zilla, let me swing that chair around so you can toast your shins by the fire. Rheumatiz acting up again? Aunt Ruby always claimed there was nothing like red flannel and carrying a raw potato in your pocket to draw the pain, though I personally think a hot footbath with two tablespoons of Coleman's mustard—oh, you haven't met my new boarder. Mrs. Trott and Miss Henbit, this is Benjamin Frankland."

Zilla said, "How do you do?"

Dittany felt a sudden mental jolt. What did she know about this stranger, except that he'd been on the mountain when John Architrave was killed? Maybe he'd been stationed there as a lookout, to keep any chance comer like herself from crossing that ridge at the fatal moment. If jolly old Sam Wallaby, who'd supposedly never done anything worse than supply the means of pickling a few livers, could be McNaster's henchman, then anyone might be anything. She acknowledged the introduction with icy hauteur.

"We've met. Minerva, Zilla and I have something to discuss with you. Could we step out to the kitchen?"

"Why, I—" Minerva gaped. She herself operated on a principle of "The more, the merrier," and was clearly at a loss to perceive why a pretty unmarried woman would take exception to the presence of an undoubtedly attractive and apparently unattached male. Frankland looked somewhat nonplussed himself, but he had the grace to back away from a potentially awkward situation.

"Glad to know you, ladies. If you'll excuse me, I'll go on up to my room and let you have your chat in peace. Don't forget I'm two games up on you, Mrs. Oakes."

"In a pig's eye you are. We still haven't pegged out on the last round. Just because you happen to be seventy-three holes ahead with only five to go, you needn't think—Dittany, quit glaring at me like that. What's got into you tonight, anyway?"

Dittany waited for the man's footsteps to get up the stairs and for the gurgle of overhead plumbing to suggest that he was in fact preparing to take his rest. Then she began her tale. As this was the third time in telling, she told it very well. Minerva was both impressed and appalled.

"And you say my Mr. Frankland was actually up there doing perk tests when it happened? He never breathed one word to me about that."

"There, see how right I was not to trust him?"

"I don't see that at all. Why should he tell me anything, just because we both happen to enjoy a game of cribbage? And furthermore, he's an honorable man."

"Oh yeah?" sneered Dittany. "So are they all, all honorable men. What about that bird who kept sneaking that oversexed doxy from Harry's Hamburger Haven up to his room and getting ketchup stains all over your best yellow sheets?"

"Do you know, I think that's the first time in my life I've ever heard them referred to as doxies in ordinary conversation," Zilla remarked, perhaps because even she thought the situation was becoming a trifle sticky.

"Dittany does have a marvelous way with words," Minerva agreed quickly, "though I myself rather incline toward 'wench.' But, Dittany, you can't possibly believe a nice man like Mr. Frankland would go shooting Mr. Architrave his second day on the job? What would be the point?"

"If he's in McNaster's pay, like Wallaby—"

"How do we know Sam Wallaby's in McNaster's pay?"

"You don't suppose McNaster's in Wallaby's, do you?"

"It seems to me one's as likely as the other. I thought I knew what was going on in this town, but now I don't feel I know anything."

"You know I'm right about getting to work on the Enchanted Mountain," said Zilla relentlessly. "How about sitting yourself down right now and drawing us a map of where the trails should go? Dittany, you might as well scoot along. We don't need you for this. Though I expect we'll be wanting you for other things," she added kindly.

"Don't do me any favors. I already have to write a speech for Samantha and a few other odds and ends. Not to mention doing a little paid work to earn my bread and butter. You can get home all right, eh, Zilla?"

"I always have so far, haven't I? Go ahead, Dittany, scat before that camomile tea wears off."

Dittany scatted. As she approached the ancestral home of the Henbits, notwithstanding Zilla's soothing potion, she began to feel herself assailed by doubt. Was she or was she not entirely happy with the prospect of having to spend the remains of what was by now a fairly advanced night all sole alone in this barny old house? By the time she'd turned her car into the driveway, she had come to the studied conclusion that she was not.

Though as a rule she wouldn't have bothered, Dittany took a long time locking the car. At last, when it became ridiculous to stand twiddling the handles any longer, she wound her way through the still leafless lilac bushes toward the back steps.

She wished there'd been a moon tonight. She wished she'd thought to buy batteries for her flashlight. She wished she'd had presence of mind enough to leave the outside light on. She was ready to settle for a brace of lightning bugs when a black shape rose out of the gloom and a sepulchral voice boomed through the darksome night.

"Avast, me hearty! Belay the lee binnacle and button up the main brace. Zounds, Henbit, what's been keeping you?"

"Arethusa," gasped Dittany, "if you're trying to give me a heart attack, you couldn't have thought of a better way. Why the avast?"

"Oh, I don't know. I was just sitting here wondering if it might be a good idea to have Lady Ermintrude shanghaied aboard a galleon."

"You're thinking of Shanghai Lil and galleons are out of the period. It would have been luggers in Sir Percy's time, wouldn't it? Once aboard the lugger and the girl is mine, and all that garbage."

"Hugger-Mugger on the Lugger? Not a bad title. I must give the subject careful thought."

"Do. Why don't you go home and sleep on it?"

"Don't be absurd." Arethusa bundled her sumptuous purple cloak (similar to the one Lady Ermintrude had been wearing when her post chaise was held up by Heartless Harold the Huntingshire Highwayman) about her and followed Dittany into the house without waiting for anything so bourgeois as an invitation. "About the end of Chapter Eleven, where Sir Percy says—"

"Not now, Arethusa."

"Stap me, do mine ears hear aright?"

"They certainly do and consider yourself stapped. I have more important matters on my mind."

"You couldn't possibly," Arethusa replied with that humility for which authors have ever been noted.

"Would you care to place a small wager on that? Arethusa, what would you say if I told you there are foul, fell deeds afoot right here in Lobelia Falls?"

"I'd say goody gumdrops and fill me in on the details before some caitiff knave swipes the plot. Unless you mean that hackneyed business about old John Architrave and the black arrow? Can't use it, pet. Stevenson beat me to the draw ages ago. Anyway, John had it coming. I might have taken a shot at him myself if I'd happened to have a black arrow about me this morning."

"This morning? Are you telling me that you were actually up on the Enchanted Mountain then? You saw him?"

"I was and I did. He was alive at the time, though. At least I think he was. I'd probably have noticed if he weren't."

"When was this exactly?"

"How would I know? What time did you go up?"

"How—" Dittany realized how pointless her question had been. Neither she nor Arethusa had any real sense of time. She settled for "Did you see anyone else?"

"No, only John. I found the spectacle unedifying and came away."

"Well, it was probably before I got there, otherwise we might have met. Anyway, I think you ought to tell Sergeant Mac-Vicar."

"What's to tell? That old John was alive before he got shot? Surely MacVicar's already deduced that for himself."

"Didn't it at least occur to you to wonder what he was doing up there?"

"No. I was wondering what I myself was doing up there."

Coming from anybody else, this statement might have sounded farfetched. Since Arethusa had said it, Dittany was inclined to take the remark at face value.

On the other hand, Arethusa was a fine strapping figure of a woman not yet fifty, who pulled a sixty-five-pound bow and shot in the gold more often than not. She was also imperious, impetuous, and a sworn enemy of the late Mr. Architrave ever since his failure to repair a leaking water main until it had washed out her formal gardens and flooded the basement she'd just converted at great expense into a paneled study and forgotten to insure against Mr. Architrave.

As for those black-banded arrows, anyone could buy a couple of new ones, maybe at that big sporting goods store in Scottsbeck where a person wouldn't be known and remembered, and paint on that theatrically ominous decoration. A person might choose a wide black band not for its histrionic eye appeal but because the person knew none of his or her friends, neighbors, casual acquaintances, or even archenemies used such an identifying mark. This would indicate a noble desire not to incriminate anybody, but it would inevitably brand John Architrave's death as premeditated murder.

And who could whip up a tastier bouillabaisse of violent demise and romantic high-mindedness than Arethusa Monk? And who else lived in such a tenuous balance between Lobelia Falls and Never-Never Land?

And who else was giving the Henbit Secretarial Service enough business to pay the taxes and buy Ethel's dog biscuit?

Surely not even Arethusa would hatch a deliberate plot to kill an old man just because he'd destroyed those magnificent plantings her great-grandmother had started with roots brought all the way from the ancestral mansion in Upper Brighton, New Brunswick, and destroyed some five thousand dollars' worth of mahogany paneling and a complete first edition of the Bobbsey Twins series that Arethusa had been collecting since her seventh birthday and might be said to have been the prime factor in molding the literary style that had brought her fame and fortune. Would she?

Oblivious of Dittany's gloomy ponderings, Arethusa tossed her elegant cloak over a chair and plunked herself down at the kitchen table. "Have at thee, varlet. Stand and deliver. Figuratively speaking, of course. You may sit if you wish."

"You're all heart, Arethusa." Dittany hesitated. But what was the point? Arethusa, though spotty in her attendance owing to sudden visitations of the literary muse, was a Grub-and-Staker in good standing and therefore sure to get the story from somebody or other anyway. "Just give me time to get us a drink. I've already told this stuff until my throat's beginning to feel as if it's lined with emery paper."

"And precisely whom have you told? No writers, I trust?"

"No, just Hazel Munson, Samantha Burberry, Zilla Trott, and Minerva Oakes so far."

"And, prithee, what do you mean so far, you fink? Or should it be finkess?"

"Arethusa, could you do me a very great favor and shut up for a minute?"

For a wonder, Arethusa did. If she wasn't hearing the tale for the first time, she was certainly putting on an impressive act. Her eyes, wide and lustrous like Lady Ermintrude's, grew wider and more lustrous with every syllable. As Dittany completed her by now well-rehearsed narrative, she drew a sigh of total rapture.

"I couldn't have thought of a better one myself!"

"Will you please try to get it through your romance-riddled cerebellum that this is real?" cried Dittany in exasperation. "Mr. Architrave's dead and we can't do anything about that, but if we don't manage to elect Samantha Burberry to the Development Commission, then Andy McNasty's going to swipe the Enchanted Mountain out from under our very noses and turn it into a housing development. I heard him say so with my own ears!"

"Whose else would you use?" said Arethusa with one of those flashes of common sense that occasionally visited her. "And you tell me yon verbose varlet Sam Wallaby is McNaster's catspaw, right?"

"Yes, and this very bilge we're drinking came from his scabrous den of iniquity," snarled Dittany, rising to hurl what was left of the sherry down the sink.

Arethusa stayed her hand. "Hold it. No fair laying a guilt trip on the poor, innocent grapes. Think of the honest peasant toes that squashed them."

"Thanks, I'd rather not. Anyway I expect there's some sort of advanced grape-squashing technology by now. How did we get switched over to grapes, anyway? Arethusa, do you have any bright ideas about the campaign?"

Arethusa pondered, her alabaster brow resting lightly on one shapely hand in an Elizabeth Barrett Browning attitude. For a long moment she sat and continued to ponder. At last she looked up, astonished. "Do you know, Dittany, for the first time in my life I can't think of a thing. Can you?"

"Well, it did cross my mind that you might like to give a donation since you're the only person I know who has any spare cash lying around. We'll need a fair amount of capital to run any sort of campaign and make a passable show of fixing up the mountain before election day."

"Gadzooks, yes. I'll endow a trash basket in loving memory of the Hunneker brothers or whatever. And you may use my name on your press releases for what that's worth. In sober retrospect, it might be worth a fair amount. I'll tell you what, I'll give that society editor who's always bugging me for an interview a call first thing tomorrow morning and bend her ear about how I go up to the Enchanted Mountain in the clear, cold light of dawn to seek my inspiration and how delighted I am that our distinguished social leader Zilla Trott—or did you say it was Minerva Oakes?"

"It's Samantha Burberry."

"Stap me! Write it down and pin it to my cloak so I shan't fluff my lines, will you? Anyway, I'll burble on about how my dear friend Samantha—you did say Samantha?—has been prevailed upon by a group of concerned citizens to lend her presence for the furtherance of a—oh, rats, I'll have to work it out on paper. Then Samantha will have to do the interview instead of me. Od's blood, I knew I'd think of something."

Arethusa tossed off the rest of her sherry, flung her cloak about her in a wide purple swirl, and vanished into the night. Dittany heaved a sigh of relief, but the sigh was premature. Before she could get the door latched Arethusa was back.

"I just thought of something else. I'll go to work on Osbert."

Before Dittany could ask, "Who's Osbert?" she was gone again.

CHAPTER 9

Dittany rather expected Arethusa to make at least one more dramatic reappearance, but she didn't. That enigmatic utterance about Osbert must have been her swan song for the night. And who was Osbert, anyway? Was he some actual being of flesh and blood who might be induced to hand out a few leaflets or hack a few trails, or was he but an Osbert of the mind, a false creation proceeding from the plot-oppressèd brain? Knowing Arethusa as she did, Dittany was inclined to the latter assumption. Sometime around the middle of August, like as not, she would come across Osbert in a heap of mangled copy paper. The prospect gave her no pleasure.

By now it was well past midnight and she was ready to drop in her tracks, had she been making any at the moment. Upstairs her comfortable bed was waiting. She yearned for that bed as Osbert would no doubt be yearning for some chaste but voluptuous knucklehead a few months from now. Yet the thought of climbing the stairs to get at it was, she might as well admit, one she did not care to entertain by herself.

There was only one thing to do, and Dittany did it. She put on her heavy storm coat, took a thick woolen muffler for reasons other than warmth. Then, somewhat embarrassedly picking up Gramp Henbit's silver-knobbed blackthorn cane in passing, she slipped out the back door again.

Avoiding the road in which some minion of Andy McNasty's might even now be lurking with evil intent, she flitted from forsythia to weigela, from *Euonymus atropurpureus* to *Philadelphus coronarius* until she reached the biggest doghouse in Lobelia Falls. Within those massively reinforced walls, confined not in durance vile but simply to keep the inhabitant from chasing skunks during the wee hours, lay deliverance. Fumbling in the dark, Dittany managed to release the heavy-duty clasp. "Ethel," she whispered. "Come on, old buddy."

Ethel came. She managed to get out just one ecstatic whoofle before Dittany, ruthlessly deft as Heartless Harold the Huntingshire Highwayman, wrapped her jaws in the muffler, led her back past the forsythia and the weigela, the burning-bush and the mock orange, and shoved her inside. Dittany's intention was to lure Ethel upstairs with dog biscuits, but the ruse proved unnecessary. Ethel was nicely tucked in before Dittany could get her own coat off.

This was probably the first time in history, not counting that inexplicable impulse of the Binkles' at the dog pound, that anybody had voluntarily sought Ethel's company, but Dittany wasn't sorry she'd done it. She'd known all along that Ethel snored and was prepared to endure the lesser annoyance for the sake of the greater good. In fact she found herself deriving a certain comfort from the sound. If Ethel could snore, then all was well on Applewood Avenue. Dittany relaxed and drifted into sleep.

She dreamed she was marching to the beat of a different drum. Something was making loud noises at her. Something huge and hairy was panting at her, exuding a peculiar halitosis that carried strong odors of dog biscuit. She stirred, opened her eyes, hastily closed them again, tried to persuade herself she was having a nightmare, then was forced to realize she wasn't. The drumbeats were caused by Ethel's tail thrashing against the blanket chest. The baying was Ethel's greeting to a glad new day and the biscuity sighs a reminder that a good hostess ought to get up and fix breakfast for her guest.

Dittany was a dognapper. Probably she should immediately phone the Binkles and confess to her crime. It did seem cruel, though, not to let them go on for another half hour or so in blissful ignorance of the fact that Ethel hadn't really been stolen. She shoved a wet muzzle out of her left eyeball, dodged a loving tongue, and reached for the bathrobe that ought to have been hanging over the footboard of the bed. It was on the floor. Ethel must have been wearing it. Dittany shook off some of the dog hairs, slipped her chilly arms into the sleeves, played hunt-the-slipper for a while and at last managed to get her warm moccasins on the right feet. Then, like Una and the lion, she and Ethel padded downstairs.

Ethel expressed a polite wish to go out. Dittany secretly hoped she'd go home to breakfast, though it did seem scrimy to begrudge a can of dog food under the circumstances. Anyway Ethel didn't choose to leave. She merely spent a discreet few minutes behind the *Taxus canadensis* and then requested to be let back in.

It was going to be another of those gray, raw, windy days. Dittany felt weary, heavy-eyed, and really not up to meeting any new challenges. Challenges, however, were just what she was about to meet. She'd barely got Ethel settled with a basinful of light refreshment when Hazel was on the telephone wanting to know if she had any expendable white sheets kicking around.

"Probably," Dittany replied. "Why? Are you setting up a first-aid station in case the campaign gets rough?"

"No, though it mightn't be such a bad idea, at that. What I had in mind was to dye them gold and cut them up for table-cloths. It would look so tacky to use mismatched cloths. By the way, you still have that bridge table and chairs of your mother's, don't you?"

"Yes, I use them in my office."

"But you can surely spare them for a day or two."

"If needs must. Anything else?"

"As a matter of fact, yes. Large casseroles, plates, cups, saucers, knives, forks, teaspoons, serving spoons, punchbowl, glasses, trays. Oh, and may we use those soapstone laundry tubs of yours to dye the sheets in? And your washer? And is your freezer very full?"

"Heavens, no. I don't even bother to plug it in, just for myself."

"Then plug it. We'll need somewhere to keep the casseroles. After we get them baked, that is. You know, what we'd best do is bring all the ingredients over to your house and get our crew together and assemble and bake them right there in your kitchen. Then we can pop them straight down cellar into the freezer. I'll do the first lot of shopping this morning and put the groceries in your pantry. That will be easiest."

"Easiest for whom?" Dittany said nastily, but Hazel only murmured something about cream of shrimp soup and hung up.

Dittany made herself some tea and a great deal of toast. She was halfway through her first slice when the telephone rang again. Zilla Trott, full of beans from a good night's rest induced no doubt by clean living and camomile tea, was also bubbling with plans. "It's all set. The Boy Scouts will be over at the mountain directly after school lets out. Got any rakes, hoes, shears—"

"Machetes, bolo knives, can openers, hatpins, buttonhooks? Sure thing, Zilla. Help yourself to whatever you can find in the tool shed."

"Can't you just load everything into your wheelbarrow and bring it along when you come?"

"What makes you think I'm coming?"

"Dittany, you've got to! We can't let those boys go yanking and snipping without supervision. You're the only one except myself and Minerva who's really sure what grows where."

"But I have to write a speech for Samantha and clear the pantry for Hazel to park her shrimp soup and find sheets to dye for tablecloths and—and besides, you're not the one who got shot at."

"Neither are you. Just because a stray arrow happened to land somewhere in your vicinity—"

"Didn't mean a thing, eh? In one ear and out the other."

"That's a gross exaggeration. Anyway, if it did come close, that's all the more reason why you need to overcome any irrational fears that may be lurking in your subconscious mind."

"Zilla, my fears are neither subconscious nor irrational."

"Then you must deal with them at once. Half past one and not a second later. Bring a ball of string and a bag of lime to mark trails with. And I'm sure you won't mind if the work crew leave their shovels and stuff in your tool shed. It will be so much—"

"I know, handier for everyone. Okay, but somebody will have to keep track of which is whose. I'm darned if I'll sort them out."

She'd also be darned if she didn't, no doubt. Groaning, Dittany hung up and took a bite of cold toast. She hadn't got round to calling the Binkles about Ethel but it was too late now. They'd have gone on their way rejoicing ages ago. Would cold toast be more palatable with jam? She was about to experiment when Therese Boulanger called.

"Dittany, can we count on your help at the bake sale?"

"What bake sale, for Pete's sake?"

"The one we're holding Saturday morning to raise funds for the Enchanted Mountain Reclamation Project. Didn't Hazel tell you?"

"I only remember soup and sheets."

"Oh, I'm glad you mentioned sheets. We'll need your grandmother's old sewing room to get them cut and hemmed. And Ellie Despard's going to make the most adorable butterfly centerpieces out of gold lace paper doilies, but she needs a space to work, so—"

"Don't tell me. Let me guess."

"Well, you do have that big house all to yourself, Dittany."

"That's what you think, Therese. Look, why don't I leave the key under the mat? You folks just march in four abreast and make yourselves at home."

"But, Dittany, we're counting on you! Where will you be?"

"Who knows? Up on the mountain catching poison ivy with Zilla, over helping Samantha memorize the speech I haven't written yet, robbing clotheslines for you and Hazel—"

"Speaking of clotheslines, is your dryer working?"

"My clothesline is."

"What if it rains?"

"It wouldn't dare."

Therese permitted herself a snicker. "Ellie said she'd do some posters for Samantha's campaign."

"Great!"

"I told her you'd show her what to put on them."

"*Merci* and a rousing *beaucoup*. What time is she coming over?"

"I expect she's on her way. She has to work while Petey's at kindergarten, you know."

Dittany knew. She'd made the mistake of offering to baby-sit Petey once. She was still quailing at the memory when Ellie arrived laden with scissors, paste pots, and sundry other items that were no doubt necessary for turning gold paper doilies into butterflies. Ellie was about to dump her messy armload on Gram Henbit's solid mahogany dining-room table when Dittany screamed.

"Ellie, wait. Let me spread something over the table before you begin slopping that gunk around."

"Dittany, you're turning into a regular old maid. Why don't you get married and find out what life's all about? Though I must say there are times when I wish I'd never learned," Ellie added rather wistfully. "Do as you please, then. I've got to run down to Mr. Gumpert's for poster board."

Ellie dumped her armload on a chair and ran off, looking flushed and chic in her plaid coat, purple pants, and lime-green jersey with bright orange paint spots on it. By the time she got back, Dittany had the table set up for work and a rough sketch ready.

"How's this for an idea, Ellie? See, you print the headline YOU HAVE A CHOICE . . . THIS . . . and you draw a few moldy-looking beer cans . . . OR THIS . . . and you put in a tree and some flowers. Then you print at the bottom WRITE IN SAMANTHA BURBERRY FOR DEVELOPMENT COMMISSION WHEN YOU VOTE TUESDAY, APRIL 2."

"It's fine," said the artist, "only you know it takes me forever to letter. I'll tell you what, why don't I draw the beer cans and you put in the words?"

"Ellie, I can't do posters!"

"You can so. You lettered every one of those seventy million signs for the flower show, didn't you?"

"Yes, but that was to get out of being on the Cleanup Committee."

"Well, this is for a higher and nobler purpose. Come on, Dittany, Lobelia Falls needs you."

"Lobelia Falls is getting too darn much of me as it is," grumbled Dittany as she plunked herself down at the table and reached for a Magic Marker. She and Ellie had their public relations assembly line rolling along nicely when Samantha called in a Grade A tizzy to say the Lobelia *Leader*'s society editor had just this minute called up to ask for an interview and what was Dittany going to do about it?

"What can I do? You're the one she—oh, all right, Samantha. What time does the balloon go up?"

"She said she'd be here at two on the dot. And I haven't even made the bed yet!"

"Samantha, I doubt very much if it will be that sort of interview. Tidy up the living room and come over here about half past eleven for a bite of lunch so we can talk over what you're to say."

By then, God willing, Hazel would be back from her shopping trip and Dittany could filch something out of the grocery bags. Otherwise, there'd be slim pickings. Dittany's thoughts about the interview were pretty slim also. She did know they'd have to be awfully careful not to mention McNaster's name in any way, shape, or form. If he found so much as a whisper of an excuse he'd have that blot on the legal escutcheon slap them with a charge of slander or whatever it was when you accused somebody of doing something rotten before he'd actually got the chance to pull it off.

Knowing her home town as she did, of course, Dittany realized that by now, which was roughly ten o'clock, every member of the club and sundry of her friends, neighbors, and third cousins twice removed had heard under vows of strictest confidence the inside story about Samantha's candidacy, and that every single one of them was out hunting up some as yet unbent ear to whisper it into.

From the campaign's point of view, that was marvelous. There was no surer way to get a listener's complete attention than to start a sentence with "You mustn't breathe a word of this, but—" From Dittany's personal angle, it wasn't so great. Sooner or later, and more probably sooner than later, word would get to the ears of Sam Wallaby that everybody involved in this sudden attack on what he'd expected to be a shoo-in election was operating out of the Henbit house. And he might remember he'd mentioned a write-in campaign as the only possible way to defeat him. And he might remember that a strange charwoman in a bright red wig had tried to gate-crash McNaster's strategy session directly after he'd said it. And how could he possibly not remember Dittany's mother's smash performance as the Madwoman of Chaillot because kindly old Sam had donated the pink champagne for the cast party afterward.

Kindly old Sam was by no means always in his liquor store. He was apt as not to leave his clerks Alf and Ralph to mind the counter while he went off to do his banking or deliver an order. And everybody knew kindly old Sam used these errands as a thin excuse to sneak in a little extra practice at roving because Sam Wallaby, for all his girth and guffaws, was one of the keenest competitors and the deadliest archers in town.

And maybe the Binkles would let Ethel sleep over again tonight.

CHAPTER 10

Dittany would have to put off worrying about getting murdered until some other time. Right now there were those posters to finish. Notwithstanding three or four more interruptions, she and Ellie Despard had half a dozen ready by eleven o'clock. They did look more than a bit homemade but, as Ellie said, theirs was a grass-roots campaign and a little extra grassiness wasn't going to hurt.

"I'll take them along and stick them in store windows downtown on my way to collect Petey. I wouldn't dare go in once I've got him with me. He could clean a place out in two minutes flat. Expect me back tomorrow morning early, eh, but probably not very bright. And for heaven's sake don't let Ethel eat those gold lace doilies because Mr. Gumpert doesn't have any more."

"Drat," said Dittany, "that reminds me, I meant to have you knock off a little art work for the flyers. We'll have to do that first thing tomorrow."

"I hope you don't expect me to spend too much more time on campaign stuff. I did promise Hazel those twenty centerpieces for the tables, plus the decorations for the table and the mantelpiece, and I can't come Thursday because Petey's going to be a pussy willow in the spring pageant and I have to be at school to put his fuzz on."

"We shall overcome," Dittany sighed, and went to ponder what she could scramble together by way of lunch since Hazel hadn't yet shown up with the groceries. She was opening a can of chicken soup when Therese Boulanger blew in carrying a heap of bedraggled white sheets and a small brown paper bag.

"Sorry I'm late," Therese panted. "They didn't have one single packet of yellow dye in the whole village and I had to go clear over to Scottsbeck for it. Shall we cut first or dye first?"

"What do you mean, 'we'?" snarled Dittany. "I've spent the morning making posters with Ellie Despard, I have to fix lunch right this minute for Samantha Burberry and brief her on what to say in the newspaper interview she's having at two o'clock this afternoon, and then meet Zilla Trott and Minerva Oakes at half past one on the Enchanted Mountain with a wheelbarrow full of marking twine. Go down cellar and mix up your dye bath, then come back and have a bite with us and kindly refrain from mentioning sheets while we eat."

"Yes, of course, Dittany. I do understand your position. I merely thought how awkward it would be for one person to handle those big things when they're wet and it's so important to keep them spread out and moving around so they don't get spotty. I've been debating whether it would be better to cut them into tablecloth size first, but I was afraid they might fray unless they're hemmed but if the thread were to pucker—"

"Therese, do me a very large favor and go away till I can think what to tell Samantha. Hazel should be along any minute now and she can give you a hand. You dye the sheets first. My mother always does."

To the best of Dittany's knowledge, the former Mrs. Henbit had never dyed a sheet in her life, much less cut one up for bridge cloths, but that was a bagatelle. What Therese needed was a precedent. If there were anything in *Robert's Rules of Order* about dyeing sheets, she'd have had them all superbly finished by now. Dittany headed her in the direction of the washtubs, gave Ethel a handful of dog biscuit for an outdoor picnic, and reached for a second can of soup. It didn't really matter what she served. Anything tasted good in somebody else's kitchen. She was throwing a checkered tablecloth over the battered oak table and wondering how many places to set when Hazel blew in and started to dump her load there.

"Don't!" shrieked Dittany. "I'm setting that table for lunch."

"Dittany," Hazel replied gently, "I'm not one to criticize, as you know, but I do think it might behoove you to watch that little habit of compulsiveness you're getting into. You wouldn't want to turn into a fussy old—"

"I doubt if I'll live long enough to be a fussy old anything. Samantha's on her way here and Therese is down cellar dyeing sheets and I can't serve in the dining room on account of Ellie's butterflies. Shove that stuff in the pantry and haul up a chair."

"Oh. I'd offer to help but you can't imagine how exhausting it is to shop for eighty people. And there's still a raft of food out in the car. I don't suppose—"

"You are correct in not supposing. Nothing's going to freeze or spoil for half an hour or so in this weather, is it? Here, have a sherry and whack yourself off a hunk of cheese while I stir the soup."

"Thanks, I will. Did I or did I not see a campaign poster for Samantha in Mr. Gumpert's window as I came past?"

"I expect you did. Ellie said she'd put them around. We made six."

"But Ellie was supposed to be making the butterflies!"

"Yes, Hazel. Have some more cheese, eh? They'll get done. Somehow."

Samantha didn't arrive until close to noon. "I'm sorry, but I couldn't get off the phone," she panted. "Everybody and his grandmother was calling up about the election."

"What did you tell them?" Dittany asked as she handed Samantha a glass of sherry with one hand and turned on the broiler over some cheese sandwiches with the other.

"It depended on who they were. This is good, Dittany. To the women's righters, I said I thought it was time we had some female representation in town government, which in fact I do. I reminded those who are always crabbing about kids and noise that Sam Wallaby had got the Development Commission to cut down those nice old trees that used to be in front of his store so he could have more parking space, which was neither necessary nor desirable since it pollutes the air and brings a gang of outsiders in here on their motorcycles throwing beer cans all over the street. I said if this was Sam Wallaby's notion of civic development it certainly wasn't mine."

"Great!"

"And naturally we're all up in arms about taxes so I got in a good lick about town projects that wind up in private hands and you can jolly well bet I cited that so-called high school annex as a prime example."

"You didn't mention McNaster by name, I hope?" Dittany gasped.

"Oh no, I was most careful not to. Joshua warned me about that. But he said I could jump on Sam Wallaby as hard as I liked because that's how you play politics unless you go in for the high-minded approach, which we don't have time for. This isn't by any chance Wallaby's sherry we're drinking?"

"I'm afraid it is," Dittany confessed, "but I shan't buy any more. Here, have the last drop in the bottle and drink confusion to your enemies, eh? And from now on we spread the word to boycott Wallaby till he either withdraws from the election or we lick the pants off him, eh?"

"Right on!" cried Therese, who wasn't used to drinking anything stronger than cambric tea with her lunch.

"Well, I don't know what you thought you needed me for, Samantha," said Dittany, rescuing the toasted sandwiches and beginning to dish up the soup. "Tell that reporter what you've told everybody else and you're all set. I must say Arethusa didn't lose any time."

"Arethusa Monk? What's she got to do with my interview?"

"Everything, naturally." Dittany explained the midnight encounter. "And she says she'll donate to the Enchanted Mountain and do whatever else she happens to think of."

"Lord have mercy!" exclaimed Hazel. "Who's to say what that woman will think of?"

"Well, that's the chance we take, eh?" said Dittany. "Eat up, everybody. As Gramp Henbit used to say, a full belly maketh a stiff upper lip."

CHAPTER 11

Samantha departed for her interview, her customary sang-froid quite restored. Hazel and Therese adjourned to the cellar for an ad hoc session on sheet dyeing. Dittany washed up the dishes, found her gardening gloves and a field mouse who was using the left one for a sleeping bag, apologized to the mouse and put on an old pair of mittens instead, loaded Gramp Henbit's wheelbarrow with every implement that came to hand, and clanked off toward the Enchanted Mountain.

She realized she was walking more slowly than usual. No doubt Zilla was right about conquering one's fears by doing what one was afraid of. Zilla hadn't seen that arrow quivering in the ash tree, or old John Architrave pinned to the ground by its mate. It was perhaps just as well that Ethel upset the wheelbarrow, appearing to enjoy the resultant clash of mattocks and shears and giving Dittany something tangible to fuss about.

Ethel at least had a lovely afternoon getting in everybody's way and barking at the Boy Scouts, who might never earn their Nature Lore badges but were putting their youthful energies to good use wresting up rotted stumps and hurling dead branches into a gully where nothing grew but the weediest of weeds. Dittany kept busy enough so that she wouldn't have time to think and was getting wobbly in the knees with fatigue by the time Minerva decreed it was too dark to work any longer.

With profound gratitude on Dittany's part and some reluctance on Ethel's, they led the rattling, squeaking wheelbarrow brigade back to the tool shed and got the gear stowed. Dittany would have been glad to collapse and put her feet up after that, but she still had to replenish her larder and get square with the

Binkles. That meant a trip to the shopping mall at the worst possible time of day.

Worse still, as she was coaxing Old Faithful along the highway she was passed at an alarming rate by a huge baby-blue car that cut in front of her so abruptly that she had a narrow escape from being forced off the road. She knew the car and she recognized its driver. That burly hulk with the bright red neck and the shiny black hair could be no other than Andrew McNaster. Had he deliberately tried to wreck her, or was this just his usual way of showing courtesy on the highway?

Anyway, he wasn't waiting to find out what happened to her. He zoomed on ahead, and as she entered Scottsbeck she saw the baby-blue car parked in front of a block of offices. He must be having an urgent conference with that slimy friend of his crooked lawyer. No doubt McNaster was perturbed at Samantha's suddenly-announced candidacy and the burst of activity up on the Enchanted Mountain. But he couldn't do anything drastic at this late date without tipping his hand and putting Sam Wallaby's chances of election down the spout. Could he?

He could if he thought of something sneaky and rotten enough, and if anybody excelled in the sneaky and rotten department, it was Andy McNasty. Well, they'd just have to maintain eternal vigilance, which reminded Dittany she mustn't forget the peace offering for the Binkles, though she wasn't really all that concerned about their wanting Ethel back.

At half past six she was ringing their doorbell, clutching a gift-wrapped bottle she'd brought from the mall. "This is by way of apology," she explained when Jane Binkle came to the door. "In case you were wondering who kidnapped Ethel last night, I'm the guilty party."

"Heavens, you don't have to apologize," said Jane. "We merely assumed our prayers had at last been answered. Far be it from me to turn down a bottle of Duff Gordon. Come in and have one with us."

"Well, just one. I don't want to butt in on your supper."

Dittany knew Jane and Henry were folk of settled habits. In

fact there wasn't much she did not know about the Binkles. She'd lived next door to them all her life and cried on Jane's shoulder when her father died, although Ditson Henbit's passing had been neither sudden nor unexpected. He'd been the middle-aged son of elderly parents when he'd taken unto himself a wife something less than half his age. Though it was claimed by some that Ditson's mortal span had been curtailed by his efforts to keep up with his young bride, nobody could say he hadn't enjoyed the experience while it lasted.

Because of their retiring natures, the Binkles were probably the only people in Lobelia Falls who still hadn't heard the full story of McNaster's perfidy. As they sipped their drinks, Dittany told it with all the trimmings. By the time she finished, Jane was gasping and Henry was gazing down thoughtfully into his half-empty glass. His initial reaction surprised both women.

"I wonder who gets John Architrave's money?"

"Why, Henry," exclaimed his wife, "whatever made you think of that?"

"Consider the facts, Jane."

Jane considered, then nodded. "Henry, no wonder you beat me three games out of five. There's that big house of John's sitting right smack cheek by jowl with McNaster's den of iniquity that used to be such a nice old inn. You took Papa and Mama and me to dinner there the day we got engaged. Do you remember, Henry?"

"I remember." Henry Binkle smiled his sweet, shy smile. "You had on one of those big floppy hats they used to wear and a pink dress with the roses I gave you pinned to your shoulder. And you were almost as pretty then as you are now."

"Why, Henry!" Jane Binkle smiled back as sweetly and shyly as her husband and reached across the chessboard to touch his sleeve.

Dittany cleared her throat. "Would you two lovebirds prefer my room to my company, eh, or might I stay and pursue this interesting train of thought for a moment? I must say it hadn't crossed my mind. Didn't Mr. Architrave have any family at all?"

"Let me think." Henry Binkle flushed a bit and folded his hands across his vest. "As you of course know, he was married for many years but never had any children."

"Typical of John, eh?" said Jane. "I expect he had some vague understanding of the general principle but never got round to applying it."

"I must say, Jane, you're getting very advanced in your views lately," her husband retorted with a twinkle that suggested their own childlessness was not due to any lack of application. "Getting back to Dittany's question, John was one of three brothers, if I'm not mistaken. He was the only one too young to go. The others didn't come back."

Dittany knew what he meant. Canadian boys of John Architrave's generation had gone to places like Vimy Ridge and Château-Thierry. There'd been sentimental songs like "Keep the Home Fires Burning" and "Roses of Picardy" that Gram's and Gramp's friends had liked to sing around the piano, and another about "Hanging on the Old Barbed Wire" that nobody ever cared to remember.

"Did either of the older boys marry before they went overseas?" she asked.

"Not that I ever heard of. Do you know, Jane?"

"I don't think so, but wasn't there a half sister who sort of went to the bad and left town? Seems to me she ran off with that red-haired masher who worked in the hardware store. I can just barely remember him."

"By George, you're right! Architrave's old man was married twice, and the second wife was a sister of Minerva Oakes's mother. Good Lord, I never thought. That makes Minerva John's stepniece or something, doesn't it? I wonder why neither of them ever mentioned the connection?"

"Who'd want to be connected with a juggins like John Architrave? Anyway, I believe he took a dim view of his father's remarrying, and an even dimmer one when his half sister disgraced the family as she did. I suppose Minerva's folks were none too happy either, if it comes to that. But anyway, if John died intestate, doesn't that make Minerva the next of kin?"

"Not if the half sister married and had children. Or if she's still alive herself, for that matter. She could be. She must have been at least ten years younger than John."

"Women who run off with hardware clerks come to sticky ends," said Jane sententiously. "Not that I'm wishing her any hard luck, but wouldn't it be lovely if Minerva came in for John's money? She's had a hard row to hoe all these years with her husband dying young and those four boys to raise by herself, and now the grandchildren to help educate. She can't have a cent to bless herself with. Any woman who has to let out her best bedroom to strangers isn't doing it for the sake of having company in the house, no matter how brave a face she puts on. You see more of Minerva than we do, Dittany. You wouldn't happen to know if she keeps in touch with any of her mother's folks?"

Dittany shook her head. "I remember being down at Mr. Gumpert's a while before Christmas. Minerva was there picking out cards and she was moaning a bit about how she needed fewer each year because so many of the old folks were dying off. I'm quite sure there's only her Aunt Nellie left down in Oshawa, and that's on her father's side, so Aunt Nellie wouldn't count. But would Mr. Architrave have had any great fortune to leave?"

"Oh, I don't suppose you'd call it a fortune," said Henry Binkle, "but he must have got something from his folks, with both his brothers gone and the sister flown the coop. And he made a week's pay out of the Water Department all these years and John was never one to chuck the dollars around, eh? Then there's the house, which must be worth something at today's prices. I don't suppose many people would care to live right there next to the inn but it's in the area that's zoned for business."

"Uh-huh, and it's not going to surprise me one particle when Andy McNasty presents himself as the long-lost heir." Dittany set down her empty glass. "And if nobody swallows that yarn he'll think of another, you mark my words. Well, I must say this has been an interesting discussion. And you won't mind my keeping Ethel with me?"

"Heavens, no!" Jane assured her. "Unless you'd rather come over and sleep in our spare room."

"If I did, half the town would probably follow me over. What with the park and the election and Samantha's anniversary party, it's wall-to-wall pandemonium at my place. Oh, and while I think of it, could you bake something for the sale on Saturday if Therese Boulanger hasn't already asked you?"

"I'll be glad to. And I expect Henry wouldn't mind keeping the books on what you're going to raise. You'll have to keep careful track of the cash or the McNaster-Wallaby crowd will be trying to run you in for embezzling, like as not. Henry's awfully good at figures."

Mr. Binkle murmured something into the back of his wife's neck and she turned a patriotic scarlet. "Henry Binkle, I don't know what's got into you tonight! Go work some of it off carrying Ethel's food out to the car for Dittany."

"Want the doghouse, too?" Mr. Binkle offered gallantly, but Dittany told him she thought she could do without it. She was a little preoccupied as she avoided Ethel's frenzied whooflings and tail-thumpings and filled a huge plastic bowl her mother had once been unlucky enough to win at a euchre party with some of the Binkle dog food.

It would indeed be nice if Minerva Oakes turned out to be an heiress. Dittany only wished she could feel a totally unalloyed joy at the possibility. Maybe she could if she'd never seen that sweet little elderly lady skewer a squirrel at a hundred paces, and if that sweet little elderly lady were less familiar with the Enchanted Mountain and less fit to spring up and down its precipitous slopes and if that sweet little elderly lady weren't so hard up for cash and didn't have all those grandchildren to educate and hadn't regarded John Architrave as such a blot on the local landscape.

Then there was the lifelong friend of that sweet little elderly lady, an even better shot, an even more agile mountaineer, and a person with somewhat primordial ideas about what you did with a bow and arrow when you ran across somebody whose guts you hated and who owned something your best buddy stood in crucial need of and wasn't likely to get unless you pushed matters along a bit. Zilla Trott had offered her services as head rubber-out of blots on the landscape should the need arise and maybe she'd been joking and maybe she hadn't. Zilla wasn't much given to levity as a rule.

"Oh, knock it off, you halfwit," Ditanny told herself crossly. "That's what comes of hanging around Arethusa Monk." She was hungry, that was the matter with her. She'd stinted herself at lunchtime in order to make sure the loaves and fishes stretched to feed the rest, and Jane hadn't thought to offer anything with the drinks because the Binkles weren't much for snacking and they'd all had more important matters on their minds. She hacked an end off the remaining scrag of cheese to gnaw on while she threw together an omelet and had just got the eggs out when the phone began its jangling.

The caller was Samantha, complaining that she'd been trying to get hold of Dittany for hours to say that the interview had gone without a hitch and that she'd thought of a few more points Dittany might use in the speech.

"What speech?" Dittany mumbled through her cheese.

"The speech you promised to write me for Candidates' Night, of course. And I've got to have it right away because once Father and Mother Burberry arrive I shan't have a minute to memorize it."

"Hold on a second." Sighing, Dittany snatched another bite of cheese and went to fetch a pad and pencil. Fifteen minutes and three pages of notes later Samantha hung up and Dittany began to make herself a salad. Then Ellie Despard was on the line wondering if she had any glue because they'd need it tomorrow for the centerpieces and Ellie hadn't remembered to buy any and she'd have to whiz straight along to the house as soon as she'd dropped Petey off because tomorrow was Alison's half day, which she'd completely forgotten until this very minute.

Dittany couldn't recall whether Alison was Ellie's daughter or her baby sitter, and wondered with a sinking feeling in her stomach what Ellie had meant by that plural pronoun in talking of the centerpieces, but she said she had some glue, hung up, and began bolting her greens like a rabbit for fear the phone would interrupt her again as of course it did.

Therese was anxious to know whether Dittany had thought to take those sheets off the clothesline and if they were too dry to iron would she please dampen them just a bit but not too much because Therese and Hazel hadn't been fussy about following the directions on the dye box since it was just for the one occasion and they were so rushed but naturally they didn't want the tablecloths coming out all spotty and was the sewing room ready and could Dittany set up the ironing board and did she think she could persuade Ellie to whip out a few posters for the bake sale at the bandstand Saturday rain or shine from ten till two?

Dittany stuffed the last crumb of cheese into her mouth and went to get the sheets.

CHAPTER 12

As she was struggling back to the house with her chilly, clammy armload of washing, Dittany heard that all too familiar peal. Mrs. Poppy had recovered her voice. She'd been trying to reach Miss Henbit most of the day but first Miss Henbit's line had been busy, then Miss Henbit hadn't been at home, then Miss Henbit's line had been busy again, and then Mrs. Poppy had had to wait until Mr. Poppy stepped out to the archery club for his evening practice because Mr. Poppy was in a very funny mood these days. Mrs. Poppy expressed the wish that she'd stayed single like some other people who could come and go as they pleased with never a worry in the world and no snide remarks thrown at them.

Dittany sighed, though not into the telephone because she didn't want to hurt Mrs. Poppy's feelings, and pawed across the table for her salad bowl.

The general thrust of the call was that Mrs. Poppy just couldn't thank Miss Henbit enough for pitching in last night, though Mrs. Poppy was clearly determined to give it the old school try. Dittany chewed lettuce as quietly as she could and made deprecating murmurs while Mrs. Poppy went on not thanking her enough. "And it was just like you, not wanting me to tell Mrs. Duckes, and she's going to send you a thank-you card as soon as she can hobble down to buy one."

"She needn't bother," Dittany groaned through her lettuce. "Truly, Mrs. Poppy, I wish you hadn't told her."

"There now, isn't that you all over, Miss Henbit, doing good by stealth as the Bible says. Don't you worry a bit, I told Mrs. Duckes you didn't want it spread around because it might hurt

your business and then where'd I be? I tried to make Mr. Poppy
see that but a person might as well talk to the lamppost. I swear
men never listen to one solitary word a woman says and I don't
blame those women down in the States for holding conventions
though I wouldn't dare say so in front of my husband because
that would be the one time in his life he'd be listening."

"No doubt," said Dittany, wishing she could reach the teakettle.

"So I told Mrs. Duckes not to breathe a word to a soul and I'm
sure she won't."

Dittany found herself unable to share Mrs. Poppy's confidence. "I hope you've made other arrangements for tonight,
because I really—"

"Now isn't that just like you to offer, but it's all taken care of,
thanks. Mrs. Duckes's sister came up on the bus from Toronto.
Not that I'd mind myself if I felt more like myself, if you get
me, but as I always say, what's a family for? Speaking of which,
I'm afraid I won't get round to you at all this week, Miss Henbit.
Mr. Poppy's put his foot down, see, and there's Janet's dress I
said I'd help her finish and—"

"That's quite all right, Mrs. Poppy." Dittany didn't care to
hear about Janet's dress. "Now you mustn't say another word or
you might lose your voice again." As if a person could be that
lucky.

By now Dittany was so full of cheese and lettuce that the idea
of an omelet had palled. She made the tea she so desperately
craved and ate the tail end of a fruitcake she'd been saving for an
emergency, because if she wasn't having one now, when would
she?

"Hah!" whispered the voice of reason. "If you think this is an
emergency, wait till Mrs. Duckes's sister tells McNaster who that
allegedly deaf woman was who did his office last night." The
woman must be there now, emptying the wastebaskets, swishing
the mop around, and no doubt getting the third degree. If she
had any sense she'd tell the simple truth: that she was from out
of town and didn't know the woman who'd gone before her.

If Dittany herself had shown a grain of intelligence she'd have lied to Mrs. Poppy and claimed she'd got somebody else to take her place. Maybe it wasn't too late. Should McNaster come banging at her door thirsting for blood, she might pretend her aunt from Ottawa had been here with a maid who spoke only Dukhobor and it was the maid who—no, that wouldn't work. She'd spoken to McNaster in English. Anyway, did she look like the sort to have an aunt with a maid from Ottawa? No, she looked like the type to go out and empty trash, especially since she was actually wearing the same holey sneakers she'd had on last night. They'd been the first things to hand, or rather to foot, when she got dressed and she'd never thought to change them.

Dittany snatched off the sneakers and flung them into the wastebasket where they should have gone ages ago. She rushed upstairs, suddenly desperate to change her appearance. What she really wanted was to take a long, hot bath, put on her favorite nightgown and go to bed; but she still had Samantha's speech to write. She compromised with a quick shower, put on a lovely lounging robe her mother had sent from Vancouver, encased her patricianly slim but plebeianly aching feet in brown kid slippers, and went back down to her office.

She didn't really expect the covetous contractor to come sneaking around her house, at least not in person and not when the neighborhood was still astir. Nevertheless she called Ethel in and made sure all the shades were drawn and herself out of firing range from any window before she sat down at her typewriter.

Once she got started, the speech wasn't hard to write. Samantha had outlined her arguments; all Dittany had to do was put them into logical order and coherent English. Long practice with Arethusa Monk's garbled prose made this a cinch. Her main problem was remembering not to interject an occasional "forsooth" or "egad."

Dittany finished a rough draft, retyped it with corrections, sat back and read her effort over, and found it good. If Samantha thought otherwise she could jolly well rewrite the speech to suit herself. Pleased with this much progress, Dittany then started extracting a few trenchant passages for the flier she and Ellie would prepare in the morning. She was absorbed in her work when she began to hear a ringing in her ears. Naturally she thought of the telephone, then realized it was the doorbell.

Was this the moment of truth? Dittany's heart plummeted past the zipper in her housecoat, straight to her brown kid slippers. Then she reflected that it might only be Hazel with a load of casserole dishes, and the Henbit fighting spirit rose again. Clutching Ethel by the collar, she went and peeked around the edge of the door.

The Lord be praised, it was casseroles! However, the arms that juggled the slippery load of Pyrex were not Hazel's but a man's and the face that peered nervously over this stack of imminent chaos was Benjamin Frankland's; ergo, the casseroles had to be Minerva Oakes's and she'd better let him in before he dropped the lot.

Dittany wasn't altogether sure whether she willed or nilled, but Ethel was delighted. Perhaps she remembered that romp on the Enchanted Mountain. Anyway, she thought this would be the perfect time for another. Dittany and Frankland spent an interesting few minutes juggling Pyrex. After that any sort of formal reception was out of the question so they sat down around the kitchen table and began eating Fig Newtons.

"So," said Frankland, stirring rather a lot of sugar into the mug of tea Dittany had given him, "you're a bunch of busy ladies."

"What makes you say that?" Dittany replied cagily.

"Well, I'm none too clear on the details. I don't know if you've noticed that habit Mrs. Oakes has of starting sentences and not finishing them?"

No, Dittany had never noticed. Minerva was not one to leave anything unfinished, especially a sentence. She must be trying her best to be discreet but not succeeding any too well or she wouldn't be starting sentences in the first place. That led to uneasy speculation as to precisely how many things Minerva might have to be discreet about. Dittany bit angrily into her Fig Newton. She was not about to reveal her thoughts about Minerva Oakes to any strange boarder just because he happened to have good teeth and strong-looking hands and an agreeable way of making himself at home without any fuss.

"Anyway," Frankland went on, "from what I can gather, your club is engineering a fiftieth anniversary party for one of your members who's running for town council in order to make the ecology safe for the Plantain-Leaved Pussytoes."

"That's the general thrust," Dittany admitted, "except that it's her in-laws' anniversary and she's running for Development Commission."

"Say, this isn't by any chance on account of me, is it? I mean, because Mr. Architrave sent me up there with that backhoe?"

"Oh, don't think we're blaming you," Dittany assured him since after all he was her guest and moreover hadn't asked her to write a speech or iron any sheets. "Actually what you did turned out to be a community service, in a sense. You see, we'd always tended to take it for granted that nobody would go messing around with the Enchanted Mountain. When you started to dig up the Spotted Pipsissewa we realized something had better be done to prevent any further outrage against our natural resources."

"What about the outrage against yourself? I don't know about you, but I still get the willies every time I think of that arrow whistling past our ears."

"Oh, that," said Dittany absently. "I daresay I should, too, if I'd had time to think about it. How are you getting on down at the job?"

"Well, we did think of lowering the water level to half staff as a token of respect for Mr. Architrave," Frankland replied, studying his hostess in some wonderment, "but nobody seemed quite sure if that was the right thing to do under the circumstances, so we're just muddling along until somebody gets around to telling us who's in charge. Sergeant MacVicar was in asking questions this morning. No flies on him, eh? I asked if he was going to turn the case over to the Mounties and he told me he'd been in touch with them as soon as he got back to the station yesterday. He's had them checking cars for a hunter with black-banded arrows in his possession, but I could tell he wasn't holding out any expectations. Unless the guy was too drunk to know what he was doing, he'd either ditch them or burn them, and if he'd been all that soused he'd either have crashed his car or been picked up for reckless driving."

"Then Sergeant MacVicar is convinced it was an out-of-town hunter?"

Frankland shrugged. "That was my impression. I could be wrong, of course. You know him better than I, Dittany. You don't mind if I call you Dittany? I mean, being shot at together constitutes an introduction of sorts, doesn't it?"

"I suppose you might say so." In spite of her mental perturbation Dittany was forced to smile. There were several things going through her mind at that moment, one being the fact that some neighbor or other must even now be wondering, Lobelia Falls being the kind of place it was, why Mr. Frankland was taking so long to deliver those utensils to Miss Henbit and whether he intended to make an honest woman of her after the casseroles were in the oven. She was rather glad he was with her, but she rather wished he'd go away.

However she had no particular cause to hint as much now that he was steering the conversation to so innocuous a subject as the Hunneker Land Grant.

"I still haven't got it straight in my head about why Mr. Architrave ordered those perk tests. Isn't the land supposed to be a park? That's the impression I got from Mrs. Oakes."

"It's as much a park as anything else, anyway," Dittany told him. "The grant is public property, deeded over to Lobelia Falls on March 27, 1893, by Elmer and Silas Hunneker."

She was off and running. It would be possible to talk about the Hunneker brothers until, with any luck, she'd bored Benjamin Frankland into going away.

Or so she thought. However, her guest didn't look bored at all. He appeared only too content to be sitting there scratching Ethel's head, asking an occasional leading question, and making drastic inroads on the Fig Newtons. As she racked her brain for more statistics, Dittany began to feel put upon. She was really awfully tired. Why didn't Frankland have sense enough to go home and let her get some rest? Why didn't the telephone ring? She'd had nothing but interruptions all day, why couldn't she have one more to break up this little party before she either collapsed from exhaustion or suffered the social stigma of being branded a fallen woman without even getting a chance to commit the impropriety?

As some philosopher once observed, it is never safe to wish for anything because one is thus placed in the vulnerable position of being apt to get it. Dittany learned the vanity of human wishes. Arethusa Monk didn't even bother to interrupt with a knock. She merely swept through the door which Dittany had foolishly neglected to lock after admitting Frankland. As usual, she was in full cry.

"Furthermore I think it would be more dynamic if in that bit where Lady Ermintrude drops her muff and the mysterious stranger—by the way, what did I call him? I can't for the life of me remember and he's about to challenge Sir Percy over the gaming tables."

"Hold on a second," groaned Dittany. "I'll get the typescript. Oh, by the way, this man with the bewildered expression is Benjamin Frankland."

"By my halidom! No relation to Sir Edward Frankland, by chance? He'd be a little out of my period but readers are delightfully uncritical, don't you find?"

Arethusa flung herself into Dittany's chair and reached for a Fig Newton. Dittany left her by now definitely unwelcome guests to sort out their periods and fled to her office. She could have sworn she knew exactly where to lay her hand on the bit of balderdash Arethusa was inquiring about, but somehow Lady Ermintrude had got mixed up with Samantha Burberry's speech. By the time she got back to the kitchen she was aghast to hear Arethusa remark, "So as I see it the logical next step is for someone to challenge McNaster over the gaming tables. Or wherever."

"Arethusa," screamed Dittany, "what are you telling him?"

"That we need a champion, of course. Some valiant knight-errant to enter the lists against that caitiff knave."

"That and what else?"

"Only what you told me. After all, Dittany, one could hardly expect a gentleman to stand stripped to his waistcoat in the gray light of dawn potting at Andy McNasty for no reason whatever, could one? Not in this crass, materialistic day and age, anyhow. There was a time when the mere word of a lady affronted—"

"Save it for the vast reading public," snarled Dittany. "Don't you know he works for the Water Department?"

"And what if he does, forsooth? Full many a noble heart may beat beneath an humble sump pump. Mayn't it, Sir Edward?"

"I suppose it might if you had a pretty strong heart and a pretty small sump pump," Frankland replied cautiously. "But what does my working for the Water Department have to do with—unless you're talking about those perk tests? Dittany, is that why you and Mrs. Oakes have been pussytoeing around trying to keep me in the dark? You think I was in cahoots with that old twit? You think we were both working either for or against this bird McNaster and that's why whoever killed Mr. Architrave tried to shoot me, too?"

"I—I don't know what I thought." Dittany slumped into a chair and let her forehead rest on her hands. "I guess I'm too tired to think at all. What do you think?"

"To be honest with you, what I think is that I deserve a kick in the pants for taking this job in the first place. Look, will you two ladies believe me if I tell you that when I came to work for your Water Department I was dumb enough to think I'd just be working for the Water Department? Now I don't know if I'm supposed to be an accomplice, a fall guy, or dead. All I can say is that I don't like being shot at and I don't like being made a fool of and I think it's time I took an open stand somewhere. I'm not much on that pistols-at-dawn stuff, but if your bunch needs somebody to help with the fetching and carrying, you can count me in."

CHAPTER 13

Now that Arethusa had spilled the beans to Ben Frankland, Dittany did what she ought to have done in the first place: went straight to Sergeant MacVicar the next morning and spoke her piece about what she'd learned at McNaster's offices. She got the expected reproof for not having told him sooner, along with a veiled hint that, while Mrs. MacVicar's quasi-official position would preclude her taking any active role in the campaign, Mrs. MacVicar might possibly have a spare pan of scones kicking around for the bake sale.

Chastened but relieved, she'd gone on about her duties, which included making posters, scrubbing yellow dye out of the washing machine, helping Ellie Despard stick wings on butterflies, and answering the seldom silent telephone when she wasn't out campaigning for Samantha, marking trails for Minerva, or scrounging card tables for Hazel. She also performed delicate diplomatic missions like convincing Zilla Trott that the Burberrys would be getting enough lecithin and magnesium sulfate in their casseroles without the addition of alfalfa sprouts and that she'd better keep off the subject of soybean oil because Hazel was rapidly coming to the boiling point, as who wasn't?

Though the weather continued to bluster and sulk, work went on apace at the Enchanted Mountain. They'd got a road of sorts cut all the way to the top now. Several of the more zealous laborers were suffering from poison ivy but they passed the calamine lotion from hand to comradely hand and kept on grubbing. Their inspiring example, plus some strenuous arm twisting of relatives and neighbors, was working fiscal wonders. Henry Binkle had already made several neat entries in the shiny new ledger that was his personal donation to the Enchanted Mountain Reclamation Project.

Harassment was expected and it came. Wednesday noontime when Dittany took the copy for Samantha's campaign booklet down to be duplicated, she saw Sam Wallaby walking away from Ye Village Stationer and Mr. Gumpert in the act of taking down the poster she and Ellie had labored over.

"Mr. Gumpert," she cried, "whatever are you doing that for?"

"Well—er—" he stammered, "it's not our policy to get involved in controversial issues."

"Then why did you let Ellie put up the poster in the first place? Who's setting your policies all of a sudden? Sam Wallaby's just been in here bending your ear, hasn't he?"

"Now, Dittany, you know we local merchants have to stick together."

"And what about your local customers? How many typewriter ribbons has Sam Wallaby bought from you lately, eh? You may be interested to know, Mr. Gumpert, that Sam Wallaby is going to get the pants beat off him next Tuesday because he's created an eyesore and a public nuisance and downgraded our main street. We're sick and tired of his shenanigans and we've started to boycott his store. Of course if you choose to identify yourself with the hoodlum element, that's up to you. I'm sure your former customers will respect your freedom of choice. Now since you choose not to be involved in controversial issues I'm sure you'd rather not print up these two thousand fliers I was going to ask you to do for Mrs. Burberry. So I'll bid you a very good day and take my business elsewhere."

"Dittany," sighed Mr. Gumpert, "you grow more like your mother every day of your life." With another uneasy glance at Wallaby's unsightly emporium, he stuck the poster back in his window.

"Thank you," said Dittany sweetly, "I knew you'd understand our point of view. Could we please have these fliers by tomorrow morning, and would you mind putting up this poster too? It's about the bake sale for the Enchanted Mountain Reclamation Project."

"Oh, that," said Mr. Gumpert, somewhat relieved. "I'll be glad to. High time something was done about the Enchanted Mountain. I was saying to my wife not long ago, it's a burning shame the way that place has been allowed to go to rack and ruin. We used to go up there and fly our kites when we were youngsters, your father and I and the rest of the bunch. Yes, that was a big thing with us boys, flying kites. I expect Mrs. Gumpert would bake something for the sale if you want me to ask her."

So there was one minor branch of the Rubicon passed, but that was only the beginning. That same afternoon when Minerva and Zilla led their myrmidons up to the Enchanted Mountain, they found all the strings they'd broken their backs to mark the paths with had come unstrung. Luckily it turned out that the Boy Scouts had got in a spot of trail-blazing practice so the markers weren't really needed after all, but it was annoying just the same.

Thursday somebody started a rumor that Samantha had been guilty of malfeasance and/or hanky-panky with the flower show funds two years ago, but as in fact it had been Mrs. MacVicar who'd served as treasurer for the event and Samantha hadn't had personal control of a single penny that rumor was rapidly and indignantly squashed and the few who'd been rash enough to spread it quailed in their boots for fear of official retaliation.

Friday morning Dittany rushed out for a fast trip to the shopping mall, only to find a strange car blocking her driveway. There was no earthly reason why it should be there since Applewood Avenue was otherwise empty on both sides, so she had to conclude this was another deliberate annoyance.

Very well, she was annoyed. "Come on, Ethel," she called. "Let's find a big, sloppy mud puddle and go wading."

While Ethel was getting her paws well mired, Dittany scattered dog biscuit all over the hood and top of the car. It happened to be a white one, so the resultant pattern of plate-sized pawprints showed up nicely. Dittany then hitched a ride to the store with Hazel and sailed through the day with a pleasant feeling of being one up on the adversary.

As darkness closed in and the car didn't go away, though, Dittany began to feel a bit edgy. Should she let Sergeant MacVicar know? Was she making too much ado about nothing? Mightn't it be a good idea to give Minerva Oakes a ring first and perhaps see what Ben Frankland thought?

Ben himself answered the phone. He thought it mightn't be a bad idea for somebody to have a look at that car and how was she fixed for Fig Newtons?

"I bought a fresh lot today," Dittany assured him.

"Good. Put on the kettle, eh? I'll be right over."

Ben was as good as his word and perhaps a shade better. "Say, that's some fancy paint job of Ethel's. I took down the car's number just in case. What's the thumping noise from down cellar?"

"Oh, just the sump pump," Dittany reassured him. "We get some seepage during the spring thaw, and the pump always thumps when it sumps."

He grinned down at her. "You wouldn't by any chance be dropping a hint? Tell you what, I'll go take a look at the pump if you'll keep an eye peeled out the front window. Holler if you see anybody coming for the car. I wouldn't mind having a word or two with that bird."

"Well, if you're sure you really want to."

Dittany left him to it before he could say he really didn't. She lurked behind the parlor curtains staring out at the empty street until, as luck would have it, the kettle started to shrill, Ethel began growling and pawing at the door, and a dark form ambled toward the car all at once. Dittany flew back to the kitchen and shouted down the cellar staircase.

"Ben, hurry! I think he's here."

He ran upstairs, wiping his hands on a rag. "You stay here, eh? Come on, Ethel."

Dittany wasn't about to miss the action. She paused only to say, "Be careful," and slop boiling water over the tea leaves in the pot, then she followed. As she reached the front door she could hear language unfit for a lady's ears. The car's owner must have discovered Ethel's artistry.

Then Ben said, "Had your eyes checked lately, mister? Don't

you realize you've left this heap blocking a private drive all day?"

The miscreant muttered something and moved to open his car door. Frankland wasn't letting him off that easily. "Mind showing me your registration? I'm curious to see if it matches the license plates."

At that, the strange man made a dive for the driver's seat, slammed the door, and gunned his motor. Frankland came back up the walk.

"I expect that's the last you'll see of him, Dittany. Do me a favor, though, and be careful about locking up tonight, eh? And keep Ethel right with you. That mightn't have been so funny if he'd found you here alone."

"I know. Let's go have our tea. I feel the need. That must have been one of McNaster's men, mustn't it? Do you think they've found out about my being in the office that night?"

"Here, let me pour that tea. You're shaking like a leaf. I wouldn't worry too much about that office business if I were you. More likely this was something to do with your being up to the neck in Mrs. Burberry's campaign. Sam Wallaby must know you live here alone and since you're a young kid he probably thought you'd scare easy. Drink your tea while it's hot. Do you good."

Dittany wasn't much used to dominant males, but she had to admit they came in handy sometimes. She drank her tea and found it, as predicted, good. Her nerves somewhat steadied, she was pouring a second cup for her guest when something thumped against the foundation of the house directly below the bay window where they were sitting.

"Now they've started throwing rocks," she giggled nervously.

"Probably a tree limb blowing down. Stand away from the window, eh? I'll go take a look."

"There's no wind tonight. Ben, don't go. It may be that man in the car, back with a gang. Let me call Sergeant MacVicar."

"Relax, Dittany. Look at Ethel. She just picked up her ears, then went back to sleep. This the outside light?"

Frankland flipped on the switch, then let himself cautiously out the back door while Dittany held her breath and prayed. A minute or so later he was back, holding something long and slender wrapped in the end of his jacket.

"Maybe you'd better give the sergeant a buzz, eh, after all? He'll want to see this."

Ben Frankland didn't have to tell Dittany what "this" was. His jacket didn't hide the wooden shaft with the wide black band painted above the gray feathers. She went to the phone and called the police station.

CHAPTER 14

"Then you heard no sound until this arrow struck the house?" Sergeant MacVicar scrutinized the lethal projectile that lay on the kitchen table among the teacups and Fig Newtons. "Yet Ethel had growled when this stranger came to collect his car from the street?"

"Oh yes, she fussed like anything and pawed at the door."

"And what were you doing at the time, Dittany?"

"I'd been watching out the front window right beside her. I believe I'd just heard the kettle come on the boil and was turning around to go make the tea when he showed up."

"Mr. Frankland was not with you?"

"No, he was down cellar fixing the sump pump. It's been making funny noises."

"It is still making noises," said Sergeant MacVicar.

"I know," said Frankland. "I hadn't actually gotten around to doing much of anything when Dittany called me upstairs. Anyway, I'm pretty sure it needs a new gasket."

"Ah. So you abandoned the task to confront the man in the car and then came back here to have your tea. Where were you sitting?"

"I was here facing the window where I always sit," said Dittany, "and Ben was there at my right where the other cup is."

"And the curtains were drawn as they are now?"

"Yes. I think I started to push them aside when I heard the noise, but then I—didn't."

"A wise decision. This light over the table was on?"

"Of course." Dittany flushed slightly. Surely Sergeant Mac-Vicar didn't suppose she and Ben had been sitting here in the dark on such short acquaintance. "It's a good strong light, too. We've always kept a hundred-watt bulb in it because Gramp liked to sit here and read the paper."

"I am cognizant of that circumstance. Therefore one might assume your shadow and Mr. Frankland's would show up well enough against the curtains."

"They certainly ought to have. The curtains are just muslin. Do you want us to sit down again so you can go out and take a look? That is, if you're—"

"I am not afraid of being shot at, if that is what you are so tactfully not saying. That is a sensible idea, Dittany. Please take your places as before and do whatever you were doing when you heard this horrendous thump."

Looking rather sheepishly at one another, Dittany and Frankland went through the motions of sipping their tea and passing the cookies back and forth. Sergeant MacVicar went outside and returned, unscathed and nodding.

"Your silhouettes are clearly visible and easily distinguished. If there had been any serious intention of shooting either one of you, I doubt not you would have been hit."

"Maybe the glass deflected the arrow," Frankland suggested uncomfortably.

"There is a fresh chip knocked out of a stone in the foundation, directly below the spot where Dittany was sitting. We may, I think, assume that was done by the arrow. Glass would not have deflected an arrow traveling with enough velocity to break stone. At the very least we should find a starring of cracks radiating from a noticeable point of contact, and we do not. Thus one might conclude that this was another random shot such as the one that narrowly missed you two on the day John Architrave was killed."

"But you don't jump to conclusions, Sergeant MacVicar," said Dittany.

"I do not, and on sober reflection I am thinking those would have had to be two almost preternaturally serendipitous random shots."

"Huh?" said Frankland.

"He means you couldn't shoot like that by accident unless you did it on purpose," explained Dittany, who was used to Sergeant MacVicar.

"Precisely," said the sergeant. "The first, or what we may deem the first arrow by virtue of its paramount importance as well perhaps as its having been loosed before the others, spitted John as neatly as a chicken on a skewer. The second arrow, or that which we have tended to regard as the second arrow, was not aimlessly loosed to fall to earth one knew not where but did instead plant itself neatly in the trunk of a not very large tree close to but not dangerously close to the spot where you were. Again it has been conjectured that the shot was meant to frighten you away, but in fact it served to call your attention to reckless shooting in the area and led to your discovery of John's body perhaps considerably sooner than would otherwise have been the case.

"Now," Sergeant MacVicar went on, warming to his hypotheses, "we have another of these theatrical black-banded arrows striking this house directly beneath a considerable expanse of lighted window at which could be seen two well-defined sitting targets. That somebody could be potting at such a window without malice aforethought is almost unthinkable. That it could have been done on purpose yet with such total ineptitude would lead one to ponder the reason anyone might employ a weapon he didn't know how to use."

"Oh, I see what you're driving at," said Frankland.

"Good. The most credible conclusion, you comprehend, is that the archer is by no means without skill. The window was meant to be missed. The shot may have been intended to call your attention to something you were meant to see, in which case it appears thus far to have failed of its purpose. It may have been, conversely, an attempt to distract your attention from something that was happening elsewhere and may in fact have done so although we do not yet know what that something might be.

"In view, however, of the petty persecutions to which you have already been subjected, not excluding today's episode of the

ill-placed automobile, I am inclined to think that the purpose of
this shot was to heighten the atmosphere of ominous portent.
Does that supposition appeal to you, Dittany?"

"Not much."

Who'd want to keep scaring her like this without hurting her,
except someone who hadn't minded plugging old John Architrave but drew the line at young Dittany Henbit? Somebody
who perhaps thought she'd seen more than she had that day on
the Enchanted Mountain? Somebody Ethel knew well enough
not to bark at if she'd sensed that person's presence out behind
the house tonight, and wouldn't have gone charging after if she'd
caught a familiar scent the day Architrave was killed. Somebody
who could move quietly and confidently on well-known terrain,
even in the dark. Somebody who could shoot accurately enough
to put an arrow close but not too close. Somebody like Minerva
Oakes, for instance, or Zilla Trott or practically anybody else
she'd ever gone roving with.

But the Wallaby-McNaster forces were working the nasty
tricks department, surely. None of her friends could be hand in
glove with that lot, because they were all slaving their heads off
to defeat Andy McNasty's foul purpose.

And how could any of them do otherwise without attracting
suspicion? As it was, not everybody had leaped full armored into
the breach. Joshua Burberry, for instance, had barely lifted a
hand to help with his wife's campaign on the paltry excuse that
he had to write a paper for the conference he'd be attending
with his father right after the party. And Dittany squirmed a bit
as she recalled how Samantha herself had balked at running
against Sam Wallaby until she was strong-armed into it, and how
puzzled Hazel and Dittany had been that the unflappable Samantha could get into such a flap about a mere family party
when she'd tackled so many bigger jobs without turning a hair.
Suppose Joshua had got involved with McNaster out of mis-
placed philosophy or something?

But why suppose anything of the sort? Dittany realized she
was in no shape to think straight now. After a hot bath and a
good long sleep, maybe her brains would unscramble. At the mo-

ment she could barely find words to thank Sergeant MacVicar, who was promising to detail a member of his doughty force to guard her slumbers through the night, and Ben Frankland, who was promising to order a new gasket for the sump pump. She bade them a frazzled farewell and went upstairs to draw her bath, only to find that Hazel had left twenty-three heads of lettuce in the tub to crisp for Samantha's party.

Perhaps Patrolman Bob or Patrolman Ray maintained nocturnal vigilance or perhaps he conked out in the porch swing and let the Archer of the Black Band bombard the house at will. Dittany neither knew nor cared. All she was aware of was that far too soon it was Saturday morning, Ethel wanted out, and she herself ought to be over at the bandstand setting up tables for the bake sale.

She hurled an anathema at the lettuces in the tub, spongebathed as best she could in the bathroom sink, and put on heavy wool pants and a Fair Isle sweater. She was soothing her nerves with a mug of tea when Ben Frankland hauled up to the back door driving Minerva's big old station wagon.

"Hi, Dittany. Mrs. Oakes told me to swing by and pick up all those cakes and pies people have been leaving here for sale. I thought you'd be champing at the bit to get started."

"Aren't you the merry little jokester?" she snarled. "Since you're so full of beans, you can start lugging out whatever's on the pantry counter except those ten dozen cupcakes with the yellow frosting. They're for the Burberrys' luncheon and not to be trifled with. Trifle! I mustn't forget those three bowls of trifle in the fridge. And the roll of white paper to cover the tables."

Therese had worked out a neat floor plan for setting up the bake sale but it never got implemented. By the time Ben and Dittany got to the bandstand, donors were already flocking around with paper plates and old stationery boxes full of coconut drop cakes and butterscotch meringues. Therese was frantically trying to price the goods while fending off would-be buyers.

"We can't start yet," she protested. "Dot Coskoff has to bring us some silver from the bank first so we can make change."

So they squeezed the tables in as best they could among the

providers and the provender. The bandstand was not the world's most convenient place to fit anything into, being dodecahedral in shape and only about twelve feet in diameter. Aesthetically it was delightful, built of wrought iron in the Later Prince Albert style, repainted in its original colors of white, pink, green and gold every third year by the Loyal Order of Owls, and standing on its own tiny plot smack in the middle of Queen Street.

Nobody who wanted to get much of anywhere in Lobelia Falls could avoid passing the bandstand, so this was the ideal spot to hold any sort of fundraiser. Local custom decreed that any group so inclined should post its intention on the library's community calendar under the appropriate date. The first name down got the honor.

Therese had dutifully checked, found as she'd expected that there were no other takers for the last Saturday in March, which would usually be too insalubrious for any event but a snowball fight, and written down the bake sale with no thought of being challenged. Dittany did get a small jolt when she happened to spy a large baby-blue car heading down Queen Street but McNaster didn't try to ram the bandstand or anything so she went on tacking clean white paper covers to the banged-up folding tables. This was no time to dither.

Though Dot Coskoff was still sorting dimes and quarters, though it still lacked fifteen minutes to ten when Mrs. Gumpert mounted the bandstand steps with a lavish donation of pumpkin spice cakes, the slavering hordes could be held back no longer. Therese wisely shelved the witty little speech she'd planned to declare the sale formally open and contented herself with refereeing the first battle over who got to buy the pumpkin cakes.

Business was all that could be desired and often a bit more. Poundcake and gingerbread were there one minute, gone the next. Date squares and fudge brownies melted away like the snows of yesteryear. Even Sam Wallaby sauntered over to purchase a frosted cake in the shape of a bunny rabbit with coconut fur and pink jelly-bean eyes. Roughly seven and a half minutes after Wallaby had gone off with his bunny, Ormerod

Burlson, Sergeant MacVicar's left-hand man, waddled up full of bluster and self-importance.

"Who's in charge here?" he roared.

"Therese Boulanger," said Dittany, who happened to be nearest.

Burlson inched his belly among the tables to where Therese was bagging chocolate chip cookies with the light of profit gleaming in her lustrous dark eyes. "Sorry, Therese. I'll have to close you up."

"Ormerod Burlson, are you out of your mind?" gasped Therese. "What are you talking about?"

"Can't sell food in the bandstand. Against regulations."

"Since when? What regulations? Everybody's been holding bake sales here since Hector was a pup, and nobody ever got stopped before."

"Well, I'm stopping you now. Get that stuff out of here or I'll have to arrest the lot of you."

"Oh yeah?" Dittany Henbit wedged her slender frame in between them, hands on her hips and blood in her eye. "Now you listen to me, you old jelly bag. If you think we don't know who put you up to this just because Sergeant MacVicar took his wife shopping over to Scottsbeck and isn't here to fire you as you richly deserve, you might as well think again. Sam Wallaby panicked when he saw how much money we were making, didn't he? So he buttonholed you and threatened to shut off the beer for the Policemen's Picnic this year if you didn't put a stop to it fast, right? And if that doesn't constitute bribery and corruption of a public officer, suppose you tell us what does, eh? If you want to arrest somebody, why aren't you over there enforcing the anti-litter law?"

Dittany pointed over to Wallaby's where, sure enough, a pimply weed on a Suzuki was in the very act of tossing an empty beer can down in the already littered parking space that had so hideously replaced the magnificent old black locust trees. "And furthermore your own wife Maude just brought these cookies, so that makes you an accessory before the fact and don't think I won't tell the judge so if you try dragging us into court. You just trot yourself back to Sam Wallaby and tell him to take his keg of beer and pour it over his head because that paunch of yours is big enough already, or I'll sick Maude on you."

Ormerod Burlson was not an abject coward or an absolute fool. He beat as dignified a retreat as the circumstances would allow, not forgetting to impound one of his wife's cookies as evidence. As things turned out he'd done the Grub-and-Stakers a favor since the incident only served to attract even more attention to the sale. People were having to stand in line to get into the bandstand and the crowd below was six deep. Caroline Pitz was down among them handing out campaign leaflets like mad, Samantha herself being at the town dump where any serious campaigner must be on the Saturday morning before a local election.

Dittany was wondering whether she ought to rush over to Ye Village Stationer and ask Mr. Gumpert to whip off a few hundred more fliers when an unmarked van with Manitoba number plates chugged down Main Street, made a fast swing around the bandstand and slowed where the crowd was thickest. A hidden hand opened the tailgate. Out leaped a huge, evil-smelling, rotten-tempered billygoat.

Without so much as waiting to be introduced, the goat started butting right and left, knocking down children who cried, women who screamed, men who yelled terrible words. Attracted by the odor of goodies, he butted a path straight up into the bandstand and had his unattractive muzzle buried in a marshmallow frosted devil's food cake before anybody quite realized what was happening.

"Get out! Shoo! Scat!" Dittany grabbed Therese's umbrella and belabored the beast around the horns and neck. Either the goat was too tough to care or Dittany, as a paid-up member of Friends of Animals, was inhibited from hitting hard enough. In any event he paid no attention whatever but finished the chocolate cake, leaving a mess of crumbs on the table, for goats are not fastidious eaters, and went on to a plate of hot cross buns.

"Do something!" Opinion on that point was unanimous, but

nobody knew what to do. The goat was so very large and so very mean. He butted Dittany, he butted Therese, he butted Dot Coskoff and almost upset the money box, he butted anybody and anything that got between him and the food. He knocked over a table and upset a banana cream pie in order to get at a tray of wheat germ and eggplant muffins that had been contributed by Zilla Trott and were not among the better sellers. The goat appeared to relish the muffins and was looking around for more when a youngish, slimmish, blondish man nobody in town had ever seen before vaulted over the bandstand railing, wrestled the goat to a clean fall, and trussed its feet together with the belt from his gray flannel slacks.

All of a sudden there were heroes galore. Several men rushed up, seized the helpless animal, and dragged it off bodily to the nearby town pound, once a confinement for stray cows and horses, now maintained mostly for auld lang syne. The youngish man took off his spectacles, attempted to wipe banana cream filling off them with the tail of his shirt, put them back on still badly smeared, took a firm grip on his beltless trousers, and melted away before anybody could regain presence of mind enough to say thank you.

"What are we going to do?" moaned Dot Coskoff. "Half of what's left here will have to be thrown away. That dratted goat either slobbered all over it or trampled it underfoot. We'll have nothing left to sell."

"Oh yes, we will," said Hazel Munson with fire in her normally placid eye. "I'm going straight over to Dittany's and get those ten dozen frosted cupcakes we made for Samantha's party."

"But what about tomorrow?" gasped Therese.

"We'll make another batch after we finish here."

"If you say so, Hazel." Therese sighed and went back to scraping banana cream off the bandstand floor.

With the excitement over and the bandstand in a shambles, the crowd showed signs of drifting away. Dittany leaped up on the railing, steadying herself by one of the curlicued uprights. "Please, everyone," she called out, "bear with us a moment.

We'll be back in business as soon as we get the mess cleaned up. Fresh merchandise is on the way. And we'll thank you to notice that this was the second attempt in about fifteen minutes to stop our sale. Now we're not going to name any names or cast any aspersions, but you all know what this sale's in aid of and you're all intelligent people, so you can draw your own conclusions, can't you? Does anybody know whose goat that is over there in the pound?"

Nobody did.

"Then it looks as if we've got two people's anonymous goats, wouldn't you say?"

That broke them up. "Atta girl, Dittany," roared a voice from the crowd. "Say, who's collecting donations?"

"Well, Caroline Pitz is right behind you handing out campaign leaflets and you'll notice they're for the candidate who supports the park. If you have any spare cash to get rid of, you might want to hand some over to her. But the best donation you or anybody else can give is to get out on Tuesday and vote for Samantha Burberry. And bring your friends and neighbors and your Uncle Louie and Aunt Sophrony with you!"

They were raking in the cash hand over fist when Roger Munson rushed up with a plateful of sugar cookies, not appearing the least bit ruffled at having his regular Saturday schedule knocked into a cocked hat.

"I've organized the kids into a cookie-baking production line," he panted. "Further contributions will be along forthwith. Got to run. I'm head man in charge of ingredient procurement."

He took off like a rocket. Dittany, seeing that Caroline was managing fine with the collections down below, stopped to deal with the cookies. She was packaging them in half dozens when a diffident voice murmured in her ear, "Er—I was wondering what you planned to do with the food that got spoiled?"

She looked up in surprise. The speaker was the unknown knight-errant who had captured the goat. His eyeglasses were now spotless and his trousers secured by a piece of clothesline carefully tied in a square knot.

"I hadn't thought," she replied in surprise. "Why?"

"Well, I—er—thought I might take it over to the goat. By way of apology, as it were."

"Why should you apologize?" said Ben Frankland, who had just returned from the pound to see if help was still needed with the tables. "Last I saw of him, he was eating your belt."

"Did you leave him any water to drink?" asked the strange man anxiously. "He might choke on the buckle or something."

"Here's the stuff for the goat," said Dittany, thrusting a boxful of orts at the strange man. "And I do want to tell you how tremendously grateful to you we all are, Mr.—er . . . Ben, why don't you drop him off at the pound, then see if you can find out who owns that goat and who was driving the truck he got out of?"

"Can't right now. I promised Mrs. Oakes I'd go back and haul brush to the dump. I just stopped to find out if you want any Fig Newtons for later."

"Don't even mention cookies to me! After this episode, I'm taking the pledge."

Ben looked so crestfallen that she added quickly, "But why don't you and Minerva drop over about half past six and split a can of beans with me? She'll be too bushed to cook."

"Great! See you then."

"What do you mean, then? Aren't you coming back at two to pick up the tables?"

"Ever thought of teaching a course in slave-driving?"

He grinned and was gone, with the unknown man beside him carrying a box of mangled apologies to the recreant but now perhaps repentant goat. Dittany went back to peddling cupcakes.

By two o'clock there wasn't a crumb left in the bandstand. Gratefully the Grub-and-Stakers folded their tablecloths, sorted out which cake tin belonged to whom, and wended their various ways. As a parting gesture, Dittany scrawled across the bake sale poster with her lipstick, "Gone to work on the mountain. Come and help!" Then she picked up the heavy money box Dot Coskoff had given her to pass on to Mr. Binkle. So far this had been quite a day.

CHAPTER 15

The first half of the day turned out to be the easy part. When Dittany got home she found Hazel already in the kitchen greasing cupcake pans and Ellie at the dining table doggedly pleating butterfly wings. Dittany greased a few pans, creased a few doilies, took the sale money over to Jane Binkle, who promised to hand it over to Henry as soon as he returned from the shop, and went home again because she'd promised on Guides' honor to help frost the cupcakes.

There she was discovered by a moppet Minerva had sent down to see if Miss Henbit had any more axes and rakes kicking around because a swarm of people had come to help and most of them hadn't thought to bring any tools. Dittany festooned herself and the child with whatever she could lay hands on and trudged up to the Enchanted Mountain, accompanied by Ethel, who had heretofore been guarding the house, the butterflies, and especially the cupcakes.

"Apace" was hardly the word for the way work was going on. The mountain literally swarmed with volunteers, some of whom even seemed to know what they were there for. Chain saws whined ferociously through dead trunks and fallen logs. A shredder was ingesting the branches and spewing them forth as wood chips that were at once snatched up and carried away to cover the newly cleared paths.

Nobody appeared nervous about the fact that a still unsolved shooting had taken place on the mountain only a few days ago, though some of the young fry kept shouting, "Duck if you see any Yank hunters." Dittany found the jest ill timed, but most of the adults were too pleased with themselves to notice.

"Just look at this," Minerva gloated, her face glowing like a hot stove despite the raw weather. "Doesn't it do your heart good?"

"It can't be doing your blood pressure much good," Dittany retorted. "Hadn't you better go home and lie down awhile, eh?"

"Time enough to lie down when they plant me six feet under. What a pity to cut down that nice little birch, but it's right in the path."

Minerva swung her hatchet and the three-inch sapling lay on the ground, sliced off slick as a whistle. That was how she'd handled the frisky squirrels that invaded her attic and the cute, fat woodchucks that invaded her lettuce bed. One simply expressed polite regret and swept them neatly out of existence. Not far from here, old John Architrave had been pinned through the body by a single perfectly placed arrow. Dittany decided to go home and frost cupcakes.

By the time Hazel and Ellie gasped at the time and rushed off, leaving her to clean up their messes, the day was far spent and so was Dittany Henbit. Thankful that Hazel had removed the lettuces from her bathtub, she bathed and changed into a skirt and pullover that didn't have yellow frosting all over them. Whatever had possessed her to invite company for supper tonight of all nights?

She was opening her can of beans when Henry Binkle phoned in wild excitement, for him, wanting to know how in the name of Little Jim they'd ever managed to raise four hundred thirty-two dollars and seventy-six cents in four hours.

"I think it was mostly the goat," Dittany told him. Then of course she had to tell him the rest because Jane hadn't mentioned any goat and what did goats know about fundraising that he didn't, eh? Before she'd got him satisfied on the finer points, somebody was thumping at her door.

"Henry, I've got to hang up now. My company's here and the beans aren't even on the stove." He'd know what she meant. Everybody in Lobelia Falls ate baked beans on toast for Saturday night supper and would have been considered eccentric if they didn't.

She was surprised to find Ben Frankland alone on the doorstep. "Where's Minerva?" was her not very tactful greeting.

"Mrs. Oakes said to tell you she's not so young as she thought she was. She's going to soak her feet in Epsom salts and watch Lawrence Welk."

"Oh. Well, come in and haul up a chair. Supper isn't ready yet because I was on the phone with Henry Binkle. Can you imagine we made well over four hundred dollars at the bake sale?"

"Sure. I can imagine anything around this town. Is it always like this?"

"If it were, we'd all have been laid out in neat rows long ago. Have some cheese while I make a salad."

She poured them each a glass of burgundy from her stepfather's sadly depleted largesse, set her beans on to heat, filled the kettle, and put what Gramp Henbit used to call the eating tools on the table. "We'll have to eat in the kitchen. The dining room's full of gold paper butterflies. And I've got twenty-seven fancy casseroles in the freezer and ten dozen frosted cupcakes in the pantry but I'd be taking my life in my hands if I tried to sneak any."

"That's what you get for having a pantry. Be nice to rip it out and turn this into a real old-fashioned country kitchen, wouldn't it? You could install knotty pine overhead cabinets and plastic counters and one of those island units in the center with an electric stove and dishwasher set into a nice, rustic butcher-block top."

Dittany was staring at Frankland in stark, horrified unbelief when the door burst open as though propelled by a blast of hot air straight from Ottawa. "Ah, just in time," caroled Arethusa Monk, executing an expert riposte in tierce at the cheese. "Two more glasses *vitement, s'il vous plaît.*"

Too stunned to wonder why Arethusa was demanding the extra glass, Dittany went back into the pantry, aghast that anybody should even think of desecrating this sacred shrine where Gram Henbit used to keep the never empty crock of hermits. When she emerged she was relieved to see not a nice butcher-block island unit but a belt made of clothesline tied in a proper square knot. Its wearer, a tallish, thinnish, blondish young man, was hovering close to the door. All at once a great light dawned.

"I know," cried Dittany. "You're Osbert."

"There, you see, Osbert," said Arethusa. "I told you she was intelligent. Osbert can't stand stupid women."

"I didn't say I can't stand them, Aunt Arethusa," he mumbled. "I said I never know what to say to them."

"If they're stupid, say whatever comes into your head. They won't understand you anyway. And quit calling me Aunt Arethusa."

"But you are my aunt," he replied. "You're my father's sister."

"Is that supposed to be my fault?"

Dittany intervened. "How's the goat, Osbert?"

"Resting comfortably, I believe. His owner came and got him. He'd been kidnapped. If you can kidnap a full-grown goat, that is. Kid being the—er—junior form."

"Osbert, shut up," said his aunt. "The word is 'abducted.' Well, Dittany, aren't you going to offer us anything to eat? Or"—she took a thoughtful pull at the burgundy she'd poured herself—"do we have to wait till you get around to inviting us? Stap me, where are your manners lately, anyhow? You haven't even introduced anybody. Let's see, this is Sir Edward Frankland of course. And this, as he keeps insisting, is my nephew Osbert Monk. I presume we all know Dittany Henbit since otherwise we shouldn't be here, should we?"

"No, Arethusa," said the beleaguered Miss Henbit. "Pour your nephew some wine while I throw a couple more plates on the table. Sit down, Osbert. Help yourself to anything you can manage to grab."

"But I thought—I mean, Aunt Arethusa gave me the distinct impression—"

"Oh, she knows I always keep open house. Ask anybody. As it happens I was a guest short. Ben here was supposed to bring his landlady but she decided to stay home and soak her feet. Besides, I'm glad you came because I never did get a chance to thank you properly for catching that goat before he wiped us out. And I hope you like beans and brown bread because that's all we've got."

Osbert blushed and said he liked beans and brown bread very much. Dittany embezzled a handful of Hazel's lettuce to eke out the salad, brought up the last bottle of burgundy, put more biscuits on the plate, and collapsed into the only unoccupied chair.

Arethusa graciously poured her a drink. Ben protectively cut her some cheese. Osbert diffidently got up and stirred the beans. Before long Dittany realized to her astonishment that she was giving a successful party.

With Arethusa around, there was never any dearth of conversation. Tonight she even let the others get in an occasional word. Ben told thrilling tales of life among the sump pumps. Osbert mentioned a sister who could play the musical glasses and waggle her ears in three-quarter time. Dittany described her mother and Bert tripping hand in hand down life's broad highway, strewing high-fashion eyewear like rose petals en route. Time flitted by on winged feet. They drank gallons of tea and ate every Fig Newton in the house. Dittany was about to poll the gathering with regard to boiling another kettle when Gram Henbit's treasured mission oak clock pulled itself together for the effort and bonged midnight.

"'Sblood," cried Arethusa, "the tocsin soundeth. Come, Osbert. Haul your dear old aunty off to beddy-byes before I turn into a pumpkin."

"Me too," said Ben. "I mean I'd better haul myself off. Another big day coming up, eh, Dittany?"

"'Big' is a feeble, not to say paltry description. I'm down on the books to leap out of bed at the crack of dawn, defrost the casseroles, pack up the butterflies and take them over to Samantha's, then spend a quiet hour or two moving furniture so we can start getting ready for the party."

"Want me to lend a hand with the furniture?"

"I'm sure you'd be welcomed with open arms."

"Whose, for instance?"

Arethusa was cocking an interested eyebrow and Dittany was

wondering if a man who could speak of tearing out pantries might yet be redeemed when Ethel leaped up from under Osbert's feet where she'd spent the evening happily cadging tidbits.

"Awoo! Awoo! Wurff! Wurff!"

"What's the matter with her?" said Ben rather crossly.

"Perhaps she hears something outside," Osbert ventured.

"Most likely a skunk," Dittany sighed. "Ben, don't let her—"

Too late. The door was open and Ethel was off.

"What's that light up on Lookout Point? Somebody must be having a—" Dittany didn't wait to finish, but grabbed her storm coat and followed Ethel. Ben did a startled double-take and followed Dittany. Osbert passed them both, traveling at a little less than the speed of light. Arethusa flung her cape about her, shouted, "Yoicks, away!" and ran a creditable fourth.

Dittany still wasn't quite sure why she was running, but she now knew Ethel did indeed have a strain of bloodhound in her. What other breed could sustain such a peculiar, mournful baying or provoke so many neighbors into flinging open their windows and yelling, "For God's sake, shut that thing up!"?

Heeding no irate outcry, Ethel forged on. She must also be part greyhound, or possibly whippet. Osbert stayed well up with her. Dittany, already exhausted, began to fade in the stretch. Ben fell back to keep her company.

"What's happening?" she panted.

"Shh! Listen."

Glad of any excuse to catch her breath and ease the stitch in her side, Dittany shushed and listened. From above came sounds of breaking glass and uncouth ribaldry, then a triumphant "Awoo!" a burst of rude Anglo-Saxon immediately translated into French to meet Canadian regulations on bilingualism, and the sound of a motor being gunned for all it was worth.

"Get back!"

Ben grabbed Dittany and yanked her back off the path seconds before a vehicle hurtled toward them. Ethel pelted behind in victorious pursuit with some trophy of the chase flapping around her muzzle. The driver had switched on his lights, since trying to negotiate that newly hacked roadway down the mountain would have been suicide without them. As the machine passed, Dittany could see it was a plain black van.

"I'll bet that's the same one they let the goat out of," she hissed.

"Could you see who was inside?" Ben asked her.

"No, they went by too fast. Here, Ethel, let's see what you've got in your mouth." She managed to secure the object. "This feels like cloth. Come on, we'd better see what's happened to Osbert."

"Hold on a second. Somebody's coming."

Then they heard a gasp that sounded like "Gadzooks" and realized Arethusa was still among the party. The three of them stormed the summit, to find Osbert with a large flashlight surveying what appeared to be the leftovers from a Roman orgy of the post-Neronian period.

"Ods bodikins," panted Arethusa. "How dear to my heart are the scenes of my childhood. This place smells like our cellar the time Dad's home brew blew up."

"Minerva will have a heart attack," wailed Dittany. "How many of them were there, for goodness' sake?"

"About sixty, from the look of all these broken bottles," said Ben.

"I only saw three," said Osbert. "Ethel caught one but he tore loose and got off in the van with the rest."

"That must be how she got the cloth in her mouth. Shine your light on this, eh?" Dittany held out her find, which appeared to be a sizable portion of somebody's rearward covering.

"Mustard yellow and catsup red with brown spots," mused Arethusa. "Perchance the varlet runs a hamburger joint. Do we know anyone named Ronald MacDonald?"

"At least we know he's got lousy taste and a broad beam," said Ben.

Osbert, having glanced at the trouser seat, winced, and averted his gaze, handed his torch to Ben. He then produced a smaller but no less efficient one from his coat pocket and began an inch-by-inch examination of the ground at a spot where the shards lay thickest.

"Come out of that, you ninny," said his aunt. "You'll cut yourself."

"No, I shan't. It's surprisingly muddy here, don't you think? Would anyone happen to have a receptacle of any sort?"

Dittany fumbled in her pocket and brought out a crumpled paper cup she'd picked up when they were tidying after the bake sale and forgotten to throw in the trash. "Will this do?"

"Admirably." Osbert smoothed out the cup as best he could, scooped some mud into it, and sniffed. "I think we ought to get the police up here before we disturb the evidence further."

"Why?" said Ben.

"Because this mud reeks of beer."

"What's it supposed to smell like? Roses? Those are beer bottles they broke, aren't they?"

"That's just the point. If you were given to smashing beer bottles in a fit of drunken revelry, which I'm sure you're not, wouldn't you prefer to drink the beer first?"

"Well, sure. Oh, I get it."

"Then, since you present a more formidable appearance than I, would you and Aunt Arethusa stay here with this splendid animal and guard the evidence while Dittany and I go back to her house and get some help?"

"What am I supposed to do if those rumscullions come back, forsooth?" demanded his aunt.

"Flap your cape and scream. They'll think you're the Wicked Witch of the North."

"Thank you, Osbert. Remind me to cut you out of my will."

"Yes, Aunt Arethusa. Wait, Dittany, I'll light the way for you."

"I've been up and down this path so often lately that I could walk it with my eyes shut."

Dittany proved her point by tripping over a root. Osbert picked her up and thenceforth kept a firm grip on her coatsleeve for which she was secretly grateful. When they got to the house, Dittany realized she hadn't got her key with her and somebody had slammed the door shut with the catch on when they made their pell-mell exit. She was about to heave a rock through the kitchen window out of exasperation when Osbert did something with the thin blade of his jackknife and they were free to enter.

Sergeant MacVicar received Dittany's frantic summons with accustomed sang-froid and told her he would proceed to the scene of the outrage as soon as he got his uniform on, and did Dittany by chance have a camera with a flash attachment? A member of his department had committed the grave error of borrowing the official photographic apparatus for other than official business over the weekend. He would be receiving the rough side of Mrs. MacVicar's tongue when he returned the camera on Monday and considerably worse than that from Sergeant MacVicar in person if he forgot to do so.

"Oddly enough, I have," said Dittany. "It's even got film and flash bulbs in. I was planning to take pictures at the Burberrys' party tomorrow because I knew Samantha would never think of it."

"Excellent. And can you also furnish some large plastic bags?"

"Tons. Mama was always buying them and then not using them because they're non-biodegradable. Anything else?"

"Sticky labels, a marking pen, empty trash cans, and a shovel."

"Yes, Sergeant MacVicar. I'll take them up in my own car. There's gas in the tank. I think."

Sergeant MacVicar told her she was a credit to her sex and rang off. Dittany and Osbert were loading Old Faithful's capacious trunk when Jane and Henry Binkle appeared in the driveway, both of them wearing coats and scarves over their sensible wool bathrobes.

"Dittany, is something the matter? We heard Ethel making a ghastly racket, then we saw lights up on the Enchanted Mountain."

"We've had vandals. Ethel chased them off. There's broken glass and beery mud and Sergeant MacVicar's on his way. So are we. Oh, Jane and Henry Binkle, this is Osbert Monk. Arethusa's up on the mountain being the Wicked Witch of the North."

"Dittany, are you sure you haven't been overdoing?" said Jane Binkle anxiously.

"I'm sure I have but what the heck? Want to come along and be material witnesses? Don't trip over the shovels getting in."

The Binkles looked at one another, then climbed in among the trash containers, the flash bulbs, the plastic bags, and Gram Henbit's old graniteware dishpan Dittany had brought along because, as she'd remarked to Osbert, you never knew.

They'd barely got up to Lookout Point when Sergeant Mac-Vicar pulled in behind them. He strode to the scene of the crime, surveyed the evidence, and delivered his awful verdict. "I see absolutely no excuse for this sort of thing whatever."

He impounded Ethel's trophy as Exhibit A, sniffed knowingly at Osbert's paper cupful of beer-soaked mud, checked over Dittany's camera with expert care, then glared sternly through the viewfinder and began snapping pictures of the broken bottles, the soggy ground, and the tire tracks made by the van.

"Now, Mr. Frankland, I will photograph you taking soil samples. We will put them in these plastic bags, which we will identify in numerical sequence using the sticky labels provided by Dittany Henbit. Jane and Henry, you will please stand close to Frankland so that you can be identified as witnesses. Miss Monk, you will be so good as to join them and control that great flapping cape so it doesn't block my view."

Ben obliged by scooping shovelfuls of the reeking earth into the plastic bags Dittany held open for him while Sergeant Mac-Vicar took pictures from various artistic angles. "Want me to take these over to the lab at the Water Department?" he offered. "I could run a soil analysis for you."

"Thank you, Mr. Frankland, but I deem it more advisable to take the samples to the RCMP at Scottsbeck. This must not be taken as a reflection on your ability to perform the requisite functions. It is merely correct police procedure. Also it forestalls the possibility of some miscreant's sneaking up behind you and committing an act of aggression while your attention is focused on your work."

"Let 'em try," said Frankland bravely, but he did not press the matter.

"And now that we have all the needed veridical evidence,"

said Sergeant MacVicar, "we might clean up this broken glass lest it pose a safety hazard to the workers who will no doubt be up here at first crack of dawn."

Even Arethusa joined in the task. "If the Book-of-the-Month Club could only see me now, gadzooks," she murmured as she sloshed a shovelful of debris into one of Dittany's trash cans.

"I'd take your picture if Sergeant MacVicar hadn't used up all the film," said Dittany, "but posterity will just have to do without. Sergeant MacVicar, what are you putting that broken glass in my car for?"

"Well, you see, Dittany, we are somewhat cramped for space down at the station, whereas you have that big house all to yourself."

"Hah! All right. I suppose you'll pinch me for impeding justice if I try to stop you. If nobody can think of anything else to load me down with, you might as well climb aboard. Jane and Henry, you're both slim and lissome, you slide in front with me. The rest of you pile in back. Somebody will have to sit on Ethel's lap, I guess."

"I'll walk Ethel home," Osbert volunteered.

"The parfit gentil knight," sneered his aunt. "He just wants to weasel out of carrying in the trash cans."

But she maligned him. Osbert was there to lug his share of shards into the cellar. Not having Arethusa's nostalgic affinity for the odor of stale beer, Dittany would have been as well pleased if he hadn't bothered. She'd extended enough hospitality for one night. It was a good deal more than high time for this party to be over.

CHAPTER 16

Getting up Sunday morning was about the fourth hardest thing Dittany Henbit had ever done in her life. She might never have made it if Hazel Munson hadn't come to make sure the casseroles were being thawed, as of course they weren't.

"I might have known I could depend on nobody but myself," she sniffed.

"But Hazel, listen!"

"Later." Hazel charged down to the freezer and began fishing out casseroles. Blear-eyed in bathrobe and boots, Dittany could only sigh and help her fish. Once Hazel and the food were out of the house, she rushed back upstairs, took a fast shower, put on the yellow wool dress she'd bought on sale at Effie's Chic Boutique because everybody was supposed to wear something golden-wedding color, and was thinking of breakfast when Ellie Despard arrived to collect the centerpieces.

"Why aren't you over setting up tables?" she demanded crossly. "How am I supposed to arrange these if I've nothing to put them on?"

"Ellie, listen!"

"Not now." Bristling with gold paper and righteous indignation, Ellie ran out, ran back, ran out, ran back, and at last ran out and stayed out. Dittany gulped a cup of tea and a stale bun she found in the fridge, got Ethel settled with water and dog food, ferried the cupcakes into Old Faithful with no mishap except a little smudged frosting, and headed for the Burberrys'.

Work was already in progress. Sam Pitz, Bill Coskoff, and others were lugging out furniture and stacking it on the side porch to be protected by tarpaulins until all the pomps of yesterday were one with Nineveh and Tyre, after which time it would all have to be lugged in again. A heap of card tables and folding chairs lay ready to be set up in the space they were making. Dittany picked up a table, noted with surprise that it was her own, and joined the fray.

Soon the place had taken on a semi-festive air. The dyed sheets, some spottiness to the contrary notwithstanding, made a cheery background for Ellie's gold centerpieces. To be sure, these proved too large for their allotted spaces and were having to get a fast wing clip with Samantha's manicure scissors, Ellie moaning that her effect was being ruined and getting assurance from anyone who could spare the breath that nobody would ever notice, which was probably the case as people so seldom do.

Out in the kitchen, Hazel and her crew were thawing casseroles in pans of water, sorting out plates and forks, and assembling salads. The prospective host and hostess themselves had gone to the airport to collect the in-laws. That was just as well. Samantha was too dithery to help much and Joshua always tended to get lost in some intellectual profundity when decisive physical action was most urgently called for.

Hazel's plan was to have everything ready and most of the helpers gone before the Burberrys returned so that it would look as though Joshua and Samantha had engineered the whole affair. Only a few would stay and help serve the luncheon. These included Dittany, Minerva, Zilla, and, oddly enough, Arethusa Monk, who could be quite useful around a kitchen as long as she kept her mind off Sir Percy. Hazel herself had vowed to hang on until the last guest was fed and the crumbs cleared away regardless of the havoc her absence would wreak in the Munson home schedule. Roger, to his everlasting credit, had not only approved his wife's decision but offered to take the kids out for hamburgers.

As zero hour approached the rooms were cleared, the tables set, the mantelpieces bedecked and the butterflies trimmed. Still Ellie was not satisfied with the effect. "It needs something," she mused. "I know, plants! Dittany, go get your African violets, quick. And Minerva's palm tree and Zilla's begonias, only don't spend more than ten minutes because they'll be here. We'll bank the plants in the bay windows for a spring garden effect. Oh, and bring some empty flowerpots for staging. And for goodness' sake hurry!"

"I haven't a hurry left in me," Dittany groaned. Nevertheless she rushed home, wrapped her cherished plants in newspapers to keep them from freezing, she hoped, tore to Minerva's for the palm tree, then burgled Zilla's house. Zilla herself was still up on the Enchanted Mountain, having been kept away from the Burberry kitchen all morning lest she try to slip something nutritious into Hazel's menu. Her magic brew of old eggshells, rabbit manure, and other things Dittany didn't care to know about had produced such magnificent specimens that Dittany got back in time with Old Faithful looking like a portable greenhouse. She and Ellie finished the staging just as Samantha and Joshua drove up with two grim-faced senior citizens. The aspects did not appear propitious.

Pretending to be some passing stranger, Dittany took her car home, then ran back for Hazel's. Roger had put in an emergency call for transportation. One of the bikes he and the kids had been planning to ride to the hamburger stand had a flat tire and he was expurgated if he was going to fix it and that went to show what happened when you started horsing around with a schedule. Hazel had said, "Yes, dear," and gone back to her casseroles.

By the time Dittany had delivered the car and heard what Roger had to say about whose home woman's place was in, she couldn't have agreed with him more. She'd have loved to go home herself but she valiantly went back to the Burberrys' and sneaked around through the back door because guests had started to arrive at the front. Hazel thrust a platter of hors d'oeuvres at her and she took them to the living room just as Mrs. Burberry, Sr., was curling a haughty lip at the display in the bay windows.

"Samantha, I cannot see why you went to such ridiculous expense buying all these hothouse plants."

Samantha froze like the proverbial bird confronted by the

proverbial cobra. Dittany thrust the platter between them and said, "Why, Mrs. Burberry, nobody buys plants. We just trade cuttings and grow our own."

"H'mph," said Mrs. Burberry, afronted at being so addressed. "I never had time for such frivolities, myself."

"No," snarled Professor Burberry, "you're always too busy with frivolities of a more pernicious sort, running to meetings, listening to idiots spouting nonsense about nothing. Botany's a useful study at any rate. What's this thing, Samantha?" He poked his cane at one of Dittany's most cherished specimens, almost upsetting the pot.

Samantha hadn't chaired a flower show committee for nothing. "Saintpaulia," she answered with a modicum of her usual poise. "It's called African violet but as anyone can see, it's really a gesneriad."

"Looks like a violet to me," sniffed Mrs. Burberry.

Luckily or not depending on one's point of view, another batch of guests arrived. The hot words Father Burberry was trying to squelch his wife with got lost in the shouting since one of the newcomers hadn't bothered to turn on his hearing aid and didn't intend to because who wanted to listen to a bunch of gabble and he didn't see why his wife had insisted on dragging him here in the first place. Samantha gritted her teeth and kept on smiling. Dittany rushed to the kitchen.

"Hazel, this is a fiasco and it hasn't even begun yet!"

"Oh, how ghastly. If only your mother were here."

To say that the former Mrs. Henbit knew how to liven up a sticky party would have been like remarking that Michelangelo had rather a knack for painting ceilings. Dittany asked herself, "What would Mum do in a case like this?" Then she knew. "Keep 'em from each other's throats if you can. I'll be right back."

Once again Dittany legged it through the back yards to Applewood Avenue. There she made a quick change, dashed out again and detoured past Zilla Trott's, where she committed another felony. She was back at the Burberrys' before any actual blood had been shed.

"Good God," gasped Hazel. "What have you done to yourself?"

"Integrated with the group. Here, dump this in the punch bowl."

Hazel eyed the bottle Dittany thrust at her with understandable misgiving. "What is it?"

"Zilla's homemade dandelion wine, vintage of 1973."

"Dittany, that stuff's practically radioactive."

"That's why I stole it. Ought to blast open a few arteries if anything can, right?"

"Well, desperate situations require desperate measures." Hazel popped the cork, added the contents to the innocuous mixture that had been prepared, took a cautious taste, looked a good deal more cheerful, and began filling cups. Dittany took one of them in her hand, burst into the living room, and struck a John Held, Jr., pose.

"Heigh-ho, everybody!"

Even the man with the malfunctioning hearing aid turned to stare at her. She was well worth the stare. Her mother had been about to try out for the lead in *Thoroughly Modern Millie* when Bert and his eyeglasses lured her to pastures new. To another had fallen the role, to Dittany had passed the costume: the bright orange dress with the long waist and the short hem and the huge yellow silk rose bobbing two points abaft the left hipbone, the bright yellow cloche that covered her down to the eyebrows, the pink silk stockings rolled below the rouged knees, the string of fake pearls that hung well below where her waist would have been if waists had been permissible in 1925.

Dittany had also inherited Gram Henbit's faculty for playing by ear any tune she'd ever heard. She flipped her pearls back over her shoulder blades, blew a kiss to Father Burberry, twirled the piano stool and began pounding out, "When Polly Walks Through the Hollyhocks in the Moonlight."

Hazel and Arethusa passed around the punch. Ten minutes later the man with the hearing aid had his volume turned up full blast. Father Burberry was singing about the man from Azusa who was known all around as a lalapalooza at playing the big bass viol. Everybody was coming in loud and clear on the "Zum, zum, zum" except one soulful-looking lady in mauve crepe who wondered whether Dittany happened to know "Alice, I'm in Wonderland Since the Day That I First Met You."

This was almost certainly not the sort of party the Burberrys had envisoned, but it was, to borrow a word from Father Burberry, a lalapalooza. One spry ancient was heard to remark that he hadn't had so much fun since the last time he'd got Mackenzie King on the ouija board. Zilla showed up to help serve lunch and was sent home for another bottle of dandelion wine. When she got back with it, a distinguished professor (emeritus) of anthropology from Acadia was wearing one of Ellie's butterflies on her head and doing a rock-and-roll version of a tribal chant from the upper Amazon to thunderous applause.

They had to hurry up and serve the meal because a movement was already afoot to fold up the card tables and clear the floor for what various members of the learned group were referring to as terpsichorean revels, with special reference to the bunny hug and the turkey trot.

"The way they're shoveling in those casseroles I slaved over, we might as well have opened a few cans of spaghetti," Hazel grumbled to Dittany, who was taking a well-deserved break for a cup of tea.

"But they're eating so fast because the food's so good, Hazel. Everyone's saying so."

"Who, for instance?"

"For instance that woman with the butterfly on her head. It's as well Ellie left early or she'd have a fit."

"Why? They're enjoying the centerpieces, aren't they? In their own way, of course." Hazel chuckled. "And let that be a lesson to me."

At that moment Samantha popped in to give Hazel a squeeze and gasp that everything was marvelous and Mother Burberry had just gone up for a second helping and this was the first time since Samantha and Josh moved into this house that she'd tasted anything without turning up her nose and leaving most of it on her plate and could Dittany please come back and provide background music while they ate their dessert and would the "Anniversary Waltz" be too corny?

"Having met your mother-in-law, I was thinking of 'Hold That Tiger,'" Dittany replied with her mouth full of cupcake, "but I'm a slave to my public. Tell 'em I'll be in as soon as I finish my tea and powder my knees."

Half an hour later the card tables were out on the porch and Joshua Burberry's eyes almost out of their sockets as he watched his parents demonstrate to the satisfaction of all present that dancing the boomps-a-daisy did in fact make any party a wow. Toward the middle of the afternoon, though, energies began to flag. In pairs and carloads the guests drifted off, joking about getting together for the Diamond Jubilee, which might well happen as they were a remarkably durable-looking lot. At last only the Burberrys and a cleanup crew were left. Mrs. Burberry, despite everything, couldn't resist a last bit of sniping.

"Well, I must say, Samantha, I didn't expect a big blowout like this. The catering and that professional entertainer you hired must have cost a young fortune."

"Gadzooks," cried Arethusa Monk, who happened to be folding bridge chairs nearby, "you don't think we did it for money? Osbert, shove these out on the porch and start bringing in some of that other stuff. The so-called professional entertainer happens to be our own, our very own Dittany Henbit, born right around the corner from you on Applewood Avenue. The meal was cooked and served by some of Samantha's friends from the Gardening and Roving Club. And I"—she snapped a chair shut with a fine theatrical whump—"am Arethusa Monk."

"Arethusa Monk who writes all those trashy romantic novels?" gasped Mother Burberry.

"Which you read by the cartload, Mildred, so quit looking so snotty," said Father Burberry. "She's got a whole closetful of them hidden in what she chooses to call her study."

"Which you sneak in and steal, and don't think I'm not on to you," his wife snarled back.

"Drat it, Mildred, a man's got to rest his intellect sometimes, doesn't he? Some of your stuff isn't all that bad, Miss Monk. Not up to Lex Laramie's westerns, of course, but—"

"What?" screamed Arethusa. "How dare you?"

"How dare he what, Aunt Arethusa?" asked Osbert, coming in with a large brass umbrella stand.

"Say my roguish regency romances aren't up to your lousy rotten westerns, that's what!"

"Yours? You mean his? He's Lex Laramie? But you called him Osbert," said Professor Burberry, who liked to get at the facts.

"Naturally I called him Osbert. Osbert is his name, Osbert Reginald Monk. I named him myself. His idiot parents wanted to call him Ralph. Lex Laramie is merely a pseudonym or nom de plume, the paltry device of a scurvy poltroon."

"But Aunt Arethusa, I couldn't write westerns under a name like Osbert Reginald Monk. I'd never get anything at all published under my right name."

"Oh, I don't know," said Father Burberry. "Some of the lighter scientific journals might not object to Osbert Reginald Monk. Why don't you try a short article for *Popular Palaeontology?*"

"I don't know anything about palaeontology."

"You don't know anything about punching cows, either," snorted Arethusa, "but that doesn't stop you from cranking out acres of bilge about ornery cayuses and lone prairies."

"And when did you last haul out your rapier and pink somebody through his well-stapped vitals, Arethusa?" said Dittany, who thought Osbert looked rather sweet and pathetic standing there clutching the umbrella stand. "Hazel wants to know where you hid those extra cup towels she told you to bring."

"Who's Hazel?" demanded Father Burberry.

"Hazel Munson. You probably knew her as Hazel Busch. She has a sister, the former Rose Busch."

"Oh yes. Married one of the Tree boys. Wasn't there another named Weigela or something of the sort?"

"You're thinking of her brother Euonymus."

"So I am. It all comes back to me now. And what does Hazel write?"

"Nothing that I know of."

"I must go and congratulate her on her restraint. Come, Mildred."

"You'd better go too, Arethusa," said Dittany. "Hazel's pretty steamed about those towels."

As the rest departed kitchenward, Osbert turned shyly to Dittany. "I wish I knew how you do it. Whenever Aunt Arethusa starts to swash, I buckle."

"Just tell her to stuff it. Would you mind untangling my pearls for me? They seem to be caught on something."

"I'm afraid I've folded them into this bridge chair. Aunt Arethusa always gets me so rattled. I think it's because she named me Osbert. Don't you think Osbert Monk is the world's most God-awful name?"

"Not compared to Henbit. At least the kids at school didn't call you Chicken Little."

"Chicken Little is better than Ozzie the Chimp. And Dittany is like the music of song around the campfire with the stars shining down from the black velvet canopy o'erhead. Would you mind terribly if I were to name my next heroine Dittany?"

His voice became dreamy. "I think I'll make her sort of smallish and slimmish, but cuddly. And she'll have blondish hair with reddish glints in it like dawn over the mesa, and cheeks like the bloom on the sage, and this perky little dimple at the corner of her mouth when she smiles her perky little smile. Of course I can't shove in a lot of slush the way Aunt Arethusa does, but maybe I could allow my hero to gaze upon her with awe and wonderment and imagine what it might be like to kiss a girl with a little dimple at the corner of her mouth."

"As a change from his horse, eh?" Dittany smiled, showing the perky little dimple at the corner of her mouth, and smoothed back the blondish hair that very well might, for all she knew, show reddish glints like dawn over the mesa. Being so well traveled, her mother and Bert might have some information on dawns over mesas, though as they weren't much for early rising it was more likely they wouldn't. "I like the awe and wonderment part, but I'm a little bothered by the bloom on the cheeks. Isn't sage either screaming red or bluish purple?"

"Good Lord, 'Riders of the Purple Sage.'" Osbert himself flushed a tasteful magenta. "Zane Grey would turn over in his grave."

"You might use yucca, or Spanish bayonet," Dittany suggested. "That has a lovely creamy white blossom."

"Yes, but yucca doesn't sound very romantic, somehow. I mean, as a hypothetical question, you understand, if I happened to clasp you in a strong, manly embrace and murmur, 'Your cheek is like the bloom on the yucca or Spanish bayonet,' would you react favorably or otherwise?"

"I do see your point. Maybe, again speaking hypothetically, you should skip the horticulture and settle for the manly embrace."

"Do you think I could get away with it? You see, what with trying to remember the difference between a pinto and a palomino and all those other technical details, I've never seemed to get around to women much. Not that I wouldn't like to, you understand. It's only that, well, I never have."

"What are you two nattering about in there?" yelled Arethusa from the kitchen. "Osbert, come and dry the cups."

"Stuff it, Aunt Arethusa." And with a steely but tender gaze fixed on some far horizon, Lex Laramie strode manfully into the sunset.

CHAPTER 17

Sometime after that, Samantha Burberry also walked into the sunset. Actually, nobody knew at what hour she disappeared. She'd been at home when Joshua and his parents drove off to catch their plane because she'd walked out to the car and kissed all three of them good-by. Several neighbors could testify to that fact. The sight of Samantha taking an affectionate farewell of her in-laws was one nobody in Lobelia Falls was likely to forget in a hurry. She'd still been there when Hazel called in a swivet to ask whether a silver tray that should have been returned to Dot Coskoff after the party was still on the premises. Samantha had promised to take the tray back to Dot herself and had in fact done so. But where she went after she'd left the Coskoffs' was the big mystery.

She might have gone home to bed. By the time she'd had a chat and a cup of tea with Dot it was getting on for ten and she'd had a spectacularly taxing weekend. But nobody had seen her walking home. Nobody phoned her after ten, so far as anyone could discover. None of the neighbors could recall seeing her bedroom lights go on and off, nor could they remember noticing that the lights had not gone on and off as would have been the customary procedure. They were all pretty exhausted by the excitement themselves.

A good many people did observe that her porch lights were still burning the next morning, and that a lamp in the back parlor was on. The circumstance elicited no immediate concern. Everybody assumed she'd spent the night there alone. With Josh away, it was natural that she'd feel safer with the place lit up. It was also natural that she'd want to sleep late because who wouldn't if they had the chance?

But at half past nine, when Dittany Henbit had been trying for the best part of an hour to get Samantha on the phone with regard to the Candidates' Night speech she was supposed to deliver that evening, doubt set in. Dittany thought maybe she'd better drop over and find out why Samantha wasn't answering. When she found the lights still on and no kimono-wrapped figure responding to her repeated rings and knocks at the door, she began to ask nervous questions. When nobody could give her an answer, she went to Sergeant MacVicar.

"It's not like Samantha, Sergeant. She knew I'd be after her about this speech. If she had to go somewhere, she'd have let me know, and she'd have turned off her lights before she left the house. Besides, where would she be? She's not down at Mr. Gumpert's or around the stores, because I've checked. She can't have driven anywhere because Joshua took their car to the airport and left it there, and I can't find anyone who gave her a lift. Con-considering"—Dittany found that her teeth were chattering —"considering Mr. Architrave's being shot and the big schemozzle with the broken beer bottles Saturday night and all, I—I wish you'd tell me I'm making something out of nothing."

Sergeant MacVicar tugged thoughtfully at the left side of his magnificent chestnut-colored walrus mustache. "Dittany, if you are being silly, we are going to make fools of ourselves together. Come."

Shortly afterward, anybody who happened to be looking out a window that faced the Burberrys' back porch would have seen Dittany Henbit's small rump being given an official, no-nonsense boost through a jimmied casement. Once inside, she opened the door for Sergeant MacVicar and they began searching.

First they shouted and got no reply. That was a relief, in a way. One of Dittany's milder imaginings had been of Samantha lying helpless on the floor all night with a broken leg. Nor did they find a corpse in a welter of gore. They didn't find much of anything. The house was in tolerable order; at least they could see no sign of a struggle. The connubial couch was made up complete with counterpane and bolster. To be sure, Samantha could have straightened the bed this morning after she'd slept in it last night. She tended to perform such tasks automatically so she wouldn't have to think about them later, unlike Dittany, who tended to think of them first and then forget to do them at all.

At Sergeant MacVicar's behest, Dittany went through Samantha's closets. The only thing she could find missing was the heather-colored tweed coat, skirt, and twin set Dot Coskoff said Samantha had been wearing when she delivered the tray. A pocketbook with about fifty dollars in cash but no house keys lay on the dresser. The inference was that Samantha had taken the keys but not her bag as one would normally do when running over to a neighbor's for a short while, and gone to the Coskoffs' and never got back.

But where could she have gone on foot at night, apparently with no money? Nothing had been open in Lobelia Falls so late Sunday evening except the inn. Samantha was hardly the type to drop in for a quick one, much less in the haunt of the enemy. There was no bus or train she could have taken anywhere. Dot had said she appeared tired but pleased at the way the party had gone, and had avowed her intention of going to bed as soon as she got home. That would have meant a walk of perhaps three minutes on a well-lighted sidewalk in a built-up neighborhood where she knew everybody and could have screamed for help if she'd been accosted.

What if she'd never got a chance to scream? What if that unmarked black van, which, come to think of it, Samantha had never seen because she'd been campaigning at the dump on the day of the bake sale and home chewing her fingernails the night of the debacle at Lookout Point, had pulled up beside her? The driver might have pretended to ask directions. Being Samantha, she'd have given a courteous answer. Being a lady, she'd have stepped over to the van rather than stand back and raise her voice in an unseemly manner. She could thus have been grabbed, silenced with a hand over her mouth or even the wad of cotton wool soaked in chloroform beloved of the Victorian mystery writers, and hustled into the closed vehicle. Once shut up in the back, she could probably have yelled her head off without being heard in the street. Dittany offered this suggestion and was dismayed when Sergeant MacVicar didn't try to josh her out of it.

"Yes, we must redouble our efforts to trace that van. You remember nothing at all except that it was painted black and had Manitoba number plates?"

"No, it was just an ordinary van. But it must be around town somewhere if it keeps popping up like this."

"Dittany, the van is probably back in Manitoba by now. However, I shall relay this new turn of events to the RCMP, with whom I have already been in consultation as you know, and shall also alert my entire staff for the search."

As Sergeant MacVicar's entire staff consisted of Ormerod Burlson and two young chaps named respectively Bob and Ray, the callup was a matter of moments. However, word spread as word always did in Lobelia Falls, and the search crew that turned out was by no means puny. Dot Coskoff naturally felt personally responsible since it had been her silver tray that precipitated Samantha's disappearance. So did Hazel Munson, as she was the one who'd borrowed the tray. Zilla Trott, Minerva Oakes, and everybody else who could spare the time started prowling through back yards and vacant lots, opening bulkheads, peering scaredly down boarded-up wells, buttonholing people and asking questions that only brought more questions.

Dittany got the bright idea of enlisting Ethel. The dog sniffed intelligently at one of Samantha's shoes, tracked her briskly to the Coskoffs', then tracked her straight back home. Dittany got excited until Ethel started for the Coskoffs' again and it became clear that she was simply following the same set of tracks back and forth. Ethel was retired from duty and Dittany went to see what was happening on the Enchanted Mountain.

Sergeant MacVicar stood atop the mound like Napoleon at Ratisbon, though his place of vantage still reeked of malt and hops. He was deploying his forces with the skill of a master tactician but getting no result. That was a relief in a way, but also a source of frustration. The day was wearing on and opening time for Candidates' Night getting closer. Dittany didn't bother beating the underbrush but went straight to the top.

"You didn't really expect to find her here, did you?"

"Now that the party is over, this is the most logical place for a member of your worthy organization to be, is it not? There is always the chance that Samantha may have chosen to relieve the tensions of recent days by a spot of physical labor, and suffered an injury."

"The same kind of injury old John Architrave suffered up here, you mean? That's what you're thinking, isn't it?"

"I see no reason to connect John's demise with Samantha's disappearance on the basis of present evidence. I confess to you, however, that I have been mulling over a theory that might have sprung from the pen of our esteemed resident authoress Arethusa Monk: namely and to wit, that Samantha is being held captive somewhere until Sam Wallaby will have had a chance to capitalize on her failure to appear at Candidates' Night. Such a failure would provide him with an opening to dismiss her attempt at a write-in campaign as frivolous and lacking in true commitment. Does that sound at all plausible to you?"

"Well, of course. Why else would they have chloroformed her and shoved her in the van?"

"Dittany, we do not know that anybody chloroformed Samantha and shoved her in a van."

"Then how did they get hold of her?"

"That is a question we may perhaps answer in due time."

"Due time! They're probably sticking toothpicks under her fingernails already. Those silly ones with cellophane frills on, from the inn."

"What for? It would hardly be necessary to torture her to make her confess she is running for office. You ladies have already plastered the town with fliers and placards to that effect."

"Do you have to stand there being Scotch? Can't you see Samantha may be in terrible danger?"

"I can see that you are indulging in a luxury we law enforcement officers cannot allow ourselves."

"Such as what?"

"Jumping to conclusions. Dittany, I have reason to believe Samantha is not in terrible danger. I grant you that she may well be in grave distress of mind and perhaps of body," Sergeant MacVicar conceded. "I agree that it is surely my bounden duty to release her from bondage if, mind you, any bondage has taken place; and to bring the malefactors to justice, assuming any malefaction is involved."

"Haven't we had enough kinds of malefacting around here already? Why should McNaster stop at a spot of kidnapping? Look at the way he and his hoods vandalized this place right here." Dittany stamped her foot for emphasis, sending up a splash of beer-laden mud. "I'm sure those horrible pants Ethel tore were his. Who else would have such gosh-awful taste?"

"We are endeavoring to trace the garment. In the meantime you may be interested to know that, as we surmised, the RCMP tests revealed this soil to be saturated with beer. We can therefore assume the bottles now stored in your cellar were in fact full before they were smashed. Hence we have sound reason to deduce the affair was no rowdy drinking party but a ruse or wile intended to discredit this area as a drawing point for persons of loose morals and disreputable habits."

"And the beer came from Wallaby's, naturally."

Sergeant MacVicar caressed his mustache again. "When I ask myself who would carry out the wanton destruction of a great deal of perfectly potable beer, I find myself thinking of a temperance zealot, a madman, or somebody who is able to purchase the beverage in quantity at low wholesale prices. You are free to draw your own inference."

Dittany drew her own inference in silence for a moment. Then she said, "Are you going to search McNaster's place?"

"I have turned the possibility over in my mind."

"Then what's keeping you?"

"On sober reflection, the endeavor would not seem potentially fruitful. Do you know how many people McNaster employs?"

"A lot more than I thought he did, anyway."

"There are twenty-three regular employees, not counting the

cleaner and the various persons who have occasion to visit the offices with reference to construction jobs, deliveries, and so forth. Considering Andrew McNaster's own temperament and habits, do you think it reasonable that every one of them would be one hundred per cent loyal to his interests, eh, especially if their employer were guilty of so flagrant a crime as imprisoning a hostage on his premises?"

"Naturally he wouldn't tell them."

"Such a secret would be hard to keep, especially in a jerry-built structure like his. You may rest assured, however, that, should other avenues of search prove fruitless, I shall write myself out a warrant and go have a look."

"And in the meantime Samantha will miss Candidates' Night and Sam Wallaby will do her in and Andy McNasty will steal our mountain. We should never have let her out of our sight. We might have known McNaster would do something ghastly like this."

"And how might we have known, eh?"

"Well, because—because he shot Mr. Architrave, I guess. Only he's never—he's always pulling dirty tricks but—I suppose the thing is, we still don't quite believe he could actually—"

"Have resorted to violence? That is a point to consider, Dittany. I suggest you consider it. Consider also that it is not yet five o'clock. The search will go on. Dinna fash yoursel', my girl."

"I'll fash mysel' if I darn well feel like it," Dittany muttered, but Sergeant MacVicar had not stayed to hear. Satisfied at last that Samantha was nowhere on the mountain, he was wending his stately way toward other avenues of search.

She poked along the path a bit. Then, worn out by the stupendous work load she'd been carrying, the strain she'd been under, and the prospect of seeing it all go down the drain in another three hours' time, Dittany did what any other red-blooded Canadian girl would have done: found herself a hard, cold boulder to sit on and had herself a good cry.

CHAPTER 18

Preoccupied with her woes and the desperate need for a tissue she'd thought she had in her coat pocket and couldn't seem to find, Dittany did not at first realize she was not alone in her grief. Then a comforting hand lay on the sleeve she'd been about to wipe her nose on in lieu of anything more refined. A warm voice said, "Hey, Dittany, what's the matter?"

She sniffled a mighty sniffle and croaked, "Hello, Ben. What are you doing here?"

"Looking for you, if you really want to know. I sort of thought you might be somewhere along about here. I mean, it's sort of our special place, eh?"

Dittany sniffled again. "What's so special?"

"Aw, come on. Don't tell me you can't remember."

Still unable to find the tissue, Dittany plied her free coat sleeve until she could get the tears out of her eyes and see where, in fact, they were. "Oh. It's where we got shot at, if that's what you mean."

"Yeah, and I grabbed you in my arms and—darn it, Dittany, you might have remembered."

Now that he mentioned it, she did remember. There was still a bruise on her wrist where he'd seized it and jerked her off her feet, and another where her behind had hit the backhoe. That had been a tender moment in one sense, but hardly the sort one cared to jot down in one's diary and mark with a baby-blue satin ribbon. If Ben thought those fading contusions heralded the start of a romantic relationship he must either remember something that had escaped her notice in the confusion of the moment or else be indulging in a spot of wishful thinking.

Anyway it was sweet of him, she supposed, only she did wish he'd chosen a time when her nose wasn't running. Furthermore this boulder wasn't big enough for the pair of them and if he kept nudging her over like this, she'd land on her bruised remembrance. Unless by some chance he was planning to clasp her to his bosom in what Lex Laramie would describe as a manly embrace.

She had an uneasy feeling Ben was about to do just that when another male voice said, "Here, Dittany, take my bandana. What the hell do you think you're up to, Frankland?"

"Why the hell don't you get lost, Monk?" came the ungracious reply. "This happens to be a private conversation."

"Stuff it," barked the new Osbert. "Ma'am, if this ornery coyote has been annoying you with his unwelcome attentions—"

"Oh, put a sock in it, eh?" Dittany blew her nose violently on the bandana, which was not a flamboyant red but a modest blue. "I'm crying because I'm tired and cold and my feet hurt and we can't find Samantha Burberry and why the heck don't we all quit yelling at each other and go have a drink?"

"Whatever you say, Dittany," said Ben, and took possession of her left arm.

"At your service, ma'am," said Osbert, and took her other arm.

Traveling under heavy escort had its advantages. As Ben and Osbert each appeared determined to outstride the other, Dittany found herself being skimmed along barely touching the ground. This odd method of locomotion was great for the feet, which were indeed excessively fatigued, though a strain on the armpits. Anyway they reached Applewood Avenue a good deal faster than she would have done under her own steam and she managed to get the kitchen table between her two knights-errant while she got out the whiskey and three tumblers.

"Here, drink up and shut up while I find us something to chew on."

Both men leaped to assist her but she snarled so ferociously, "Sit down," that they fell back in their chairs and sought nepenthe in Seagram's.

"Say, Dittany," Ben ventured after he'd spent a few moments glaring in silence at Osbert Monk, who merely gazed back with the stern detachment of one who has looked long on distant horizons, "you've been rustling the grub for me a lot lately. How about letting me take you out to the inn for supper, eh?"

"The inn?" shrieked Dittany. "I wouldn't set foot in that den of iniquity if you roped and hog-tied me. Sorry, Ben, I'm sure you meant well but maybe you don't know Andy McNasty owns the place."

"Well then, is there a place around here McNaster doesn't own? Or how about driving over to Scottsbeck?"

"Ben, I can't go anywhere. If Samantha hasn't turned up by eight o'clock, I'm going to march myself over to Candidates' Night and deliver her speech myself."

"But you can't!"

"Why can't I? I wrote it, didn't I? Now I'm going to throw some bacon and eggs in the pan. After we eat, we can go back to hunting. She's got to be somewhere."

"Yeah, like for instance Saskatchewan. Dittany, I hate to throw cold water—"

"Then don't," barked Osbert. "Dittany, park yourself at this table and have your drink. You're plumb tuckered out, not to mention beat to the socks. I'll cook the bacon and eggs. They're the only things I can cook," he added with wistful candor. "Is this the frying pan you use?"

"No, take the big one hanging by the stove."

Dittany abandoned the fight to stave off this ill-timed onslaught of gallantry and tried not to notice how Osbert was dribbling egg white all over her stove while Ben cut her cheese enough to sustain a starving wolverine and kept trying to ply her with more whiskey than she could handle in a month.

"Come on, Dittany, it's good for what ails you."

"If I take one more sip I'll be drunk as a skunk. Go get some plates and things out of the pantry if you want something to do. The bread's in the breadbox and the butter's in the fridge. And if you're going to open those pickles, for Pete's sake hold the jar right side up. How are those eggs coming, Osbert?"

"Just about set. How do you like yours?"

"Any way I can get them. I'm starved."

"I'll have mine flipped, Monk. Without breaking the yolks," Ben added vindictively.

"You're just saying that because you think I can't do it."

Osbert essayed the all but impossible task and proved to Ben's unconcealed glee that he couldn't. He did achieve a drinkable pot of tea and managed to get the bacon and eggs on the plates with no serious mishap. They ate in an atmosphere somewhat less charged with male hostility, or so it seemed to Dittany, who was by now pleasantly numbed with fatigue and whiskey. As the hot food sobered her up and restored her vigor, though, she began to chafe at the bit again.

"Eat up, you two. We've got to get back on the trail."

"Dittany, at least half the town must be out hunting for Mrs. Burberry right this minute," Osbert reminded her gently.

"I don't care if they've flown in a regiment from Toronto. I have this premonition that one way or another I'll wind up having to track her down myself. I suppose it's because every last thing that's been done since I caught Ben digging up the Spotted Pipsissewa has somehow wound up in my lap. Now who's at the door? Go see, will you, Osbert? It's probably your Aunt Arethusa wanting to borrow a butt of Malmsey."

She was wrong. It was Sergeant MacVicar, looking a good deal more self-satisfied than the circumstances would appear to warrant.

"Have you found Samantha?" Dittany gasped.

"No," he replied, "but I have found a gasket that I believe will fit your sump pump."

"Who the heck cares about gaskets at a time like this? Anyway, Ben said he'd order one."

"He has not yet done so, however."

"Some information network you've got around here," grunted Frankland, a bit red in the face. "I thought I could pick one up over in Scottsbeck, but I've been so busy around here—"

"Ah, yes. So have we all, and there is still work to be done.

Put on your coats, if you please. Deputy Monk, you are prepared for active duty, I trust?"

"Yes, sir," said Osbert smartly, stuffing the last of his bacon in his mouth and doing a fast cleanup job with a serviette.

"Him a deputy?" Ben Frankland snorted.

"Mr. Monk most kindly volunteered to be deputized on the grounds that he could charge off the experience as research and thus not require to be paid out of town funds. He has already done admirable work.

"Such as what, eh?"

"Tracking down a material witness, for one thing."

"Somebody who knows where Samantha is?" cried Dittany.

"No, somebody who has provided information concerning the death of John Architrave."

"You mean you know who took those pot shots at Dittany and me?" Frankland clenched his large fists. "Wait till I get my hands on him!"

"You will perhaps not feel so eager when you hear the name of the culprit."

Dittany felt sick to her stomach. Then it must be Minerva Oakes. Whom else around here had Ben had time to get fond of? She did happen to think of one other person he seemed to have warmed up to pretty fast, and put on her storm coat before he and Osbert could start fighting over which of them got to hold it for her. "Never mind that now," she snapped. "Where are you taking us?"

"To fetch Samantha Burberry, of course. Do you not realize we have but an hour to Candidates' Night? Come, Dittany, do not loiter."

Sergeant MacVicar marshaled his posse down Applewood Avenue to Queen Street and took a purposeful left turn. At first Dittany thought they were heading for Ye Village Stationer.

"Sergeant, surely you don't mean Mr. Gumpert has her?"

"I do not."

"Then Sam Wallaby?"

"No. He insisted on having his place searched, naturally. Sam is no fool."

"Unlike some people I could mention," muttered Ben. Since neither he nor Osbert was willing to let the other walk unchaperoned beside Dittany, the three of them were marching in solid phalanx behind their leader. As they passed the bandstand and the last of the shops, they began to hear faint but raucous strains from a rock band.

"Oh, I get it. Old Blood and Guts here thinks she's at the inn. He's nuts. They couldn't keep a hostage in a place like that."

"Please maintain a respectful attitude toward my superior officer or I shall be required to take official action," said Deputy Monk.

Frankland began to breathe heavily through his nostrils. Partly to prevent bloodshed and partly because the truth had hit her straight between the eyes, Dittany intervened.

"Of course she's not at the inn! She's next door, in that big empty house of Mr. Architrave's. Why on earth didn't we think of it sooner?"

"I thought of it straight off," said Ben. "I even started over here after I got off work, but I overheard some people saying they'd got in and searched the place from cellar to chimney without finding hide nor hair of her. I'm afraid this is another false alarm, Sergeant."

"Indeed, Mr. Frankland? And who were these people you heard talking?"

"Sorry, I can't tell you that. I've only been in town a week."

"So you have. Then it is possible the information to which you allude was a deliberate attempt to mislead. I think we will proceed. Let us maintain vigilance. A guard may be posted inside the house."

"If there is one, I could knock his block off," Frankland offered, "and Monk here could write about it afterward."

"Honestly," said Dittany, "I don't know what's got into you two all of a sudden. You were pally enough Saturday night."

"Yeah," said Ben, "and then he started his bloom-on-the-sage routine yesterday at the Burberrys' while I was straining my guts out moving the piano."

"Not the sage," said Osbert. "The yucca or Spanish bayonet.

And I was laboring under the delusion at the time that Miss Henbit and I were having a private conversation."

"Both of you," said Dittany, "stuff it."

Ben stilled the acrimonious retort that was obviously rising to his lips. Trying to look nonchalant, they sauntered on past the flashing neon sign that disfigured what had once been a decent little country inn, toward the Architrave house. This was another Victorian hulk like the Burberrys' but ill kept and now wearing the bleak, deserted aspect appropriate to its present condition.

"Ugh," said Dittany. "It looks haunted already. Have you your jackknife, Osbert? He's awfully clever at burglary," she explained to Sergeant MacVicar, "or shouldn't I have said that?"

All the sergeant replied was, "Let's go around to the back and give it a try."

They found the rear entrance, well screened by overgrown lilacs, and Osbert tried his skill on the catch. After having looked on impatiently for a moment, Ben brushed him roughly aside.

"Okay, you've played long enough. I'll smash it in with my shoulder."

"Do," said Osbert.

Ben heaved his bulk against the paneling. He had failed to observe that Osbert's effort to open the door had already succeeded.

As he struggled to get up off the entryway floor, he roared, "You did that on purpose," if one can be said to roar in a hoarse whisper.

"Of course I did," Osbert hissed back. "You watched me, didn't you? Did you bring a flashlight?"

"No," growled Ben.

"Fortunately I came prepared."

"In point of fact, the electricity is still working." Sergeant MacVicar switched on a light, to reveal as depressing a welter of broken-down furniture, dirt, and cobwebs as the most Dickensian imagination could conjure up. "Oh, my! This will present a problem for whoever finally inherits. You will perhaps be interested to know that we have traced John's sister. She met her demise some time back in an auto crash with the man who may or may not have been her third husband."

"But what happened to the child Aunt Arethusa says she was —er—" Osbert cast an embarrassed glance at Dittany, for writers of western stories are a pure-minded lot who do not lightly toss around words like "pregnant" in the presence of unmarried ladies.

"What happened to Samantha?" she retorted, sticking tenaciously to the point from which these perverse males showed such a regrettable tendency to stray. "Let's look upstairs. If they have any common decency they'd at least put her near the bathroom."

"Okay, you do that," said Ben. "Monk here can look downstairs and I'll check the cellar."

"We will all stay together," said Sergeant MacVicar. "Who knows what evils lurk in the heart of her captor?"

Whatever evils might lurk, they were apparently not to be molested by. They poked without interference through the hideous rooms together. The downstairs was a mess, but it at least looked as if somebody had lived there. Three of the four bedrooms upstairs were furnished only in dust and mildew. Architrave had used the fourth, and it was not pleasant to see his crumpled shirts and soiled long johns thrown about the floor.

The attic was hopeless: never floored over properly and strewn with junk. There was, Dittany was relieved to see, no trunk big enough to hold a body. That left only the dirt cellar and there they found Samantha, bound and gagged and thrown into the coalbin, her handsome face gray with dirt and exhaustion, streaked with tears of thanksgiving as they loosened the gag and the ropes that had kept her helpless.

At first she couldn't even talk, only laugh and cry hysterically at the same time. They rubbed her arms and legs until the blood was circulating freely again, then got her upstairs to the bathroom. By then, with Dittany's help, she managed to pull herself together, drink several glasses of water to wash down the coal dust and the taste of the gag, sponge some of the grime off her face, and use, with ineffable gratitude, the facilities.

Luckily nobody had got around to disconnecting Mr. Architrave's phone. Sergeant MacVicar called his wife to request that she put out an all-points bulletin to the effect that the lost had been found and dispatch Bob and Ray forthwith in the police cruiser to pick up Samantha. In the meantime Dittany rooted around the old man's kitchen, managed to find a packet of tea, boiled a kettle, and washed a cup. The hot drink and a few stale crackers, which were all Architrave's larder afforded, revived Samantha enough so that she could tell her story. It didn't take long.

"All I know is that I'd been over returning that silver tray of Dot Coskoff's. You know about that, I expect. I suppose I should have known better than to go out alone after dark with things being as they are, but I was still keyed up from the party and felt a walk would do me good, and I just didn't think. Anyway, it was just around the corner. I never dreamed anything could happen in so short a distance."

Samantha took another swallow of the black, sweet tea. "But as I was going back up our own walk coming home from Dot's, I heard what I thought was a child crying in the shrubbery around to the side. I thought it might be that little imp of Ellie Despard's up to his tricks again. You remember the time Petey shinned down their porch pillars in his Doctor Dentons and almost froze to death because everybody in town was watching that Lex Laramie special on television and we couldn't hear him yelling? So anyway, I started to look for him, then somebody clapped a hand over my mouth and started pulling on my scarf. I suppose it was the same person who'd been making the noises to attract my attention. I thought sure I was being strangled, but apparently I wasn't."

"No doubt the miscreant was merely cutting off your breath so that you would lose consciousness," said Sergeant MacVicar. "It was adroitly done. You were probably then drugged."

"I think I must have been, because I don't remember anything else until I came to in that filthy coalbin with the most God-awful headache and with my hands and feet tied and that rag or whatever it was in my mouth. And after that I kept dropping off to sleep again, I believe. It's all foggy. I've no idea how long I've been here."

"Approximately twenty-two hours, so far as we are able to ascertain without further information," said Sergeant MacVicar.

"Twenty-two hours! Then it's Monday night and we've missed Candidates' Night!"

"No, we haven't," said Dittany. "My watch says two minutes of eight."

"Then what are we fooling around here for? Come on!"

"Mrs. Burberry, you're not fit," Ben objected.

"In a pig's eye I'm not. You get me over to that auditorium if you have to carry me in a basket."

"Don't you at least want to get cleaned up first?"

"Don't I ever! But they're going to see me just the way I am so they'll know that skunk for exactly what he is. Oh, but I am so hungry."

"They won't start on the dot, they never do," said Dittany. "Here's the police car now. We'll stop at my place just long enough to get some soup into you."

"And while you are doing that," said Sergeant MacVicar, "my lads can be loading those trash cans full of broken beer bottles into the cruiser. Since you are putting on such a valiant show, Samantha, you may as well give them a smashing encore."

CHAPTER 19

To say that Samantha Burberry created a sensation when she staggered into the auditorium fifteen minutes late under heavy police escort and covered with coal dust would be to utter the understatement of all time. The meeting had already been called to order, but it had to be called again and then a third time when Sergeant MacVicar and his myrmidons (including Ben, whom he had deputized for the occasion over Frankland's modest protests), having deposited Samantha in a chair handy to the tea and buns so she could finish her impromptu repast, went back outside and returned, each rolling a trash barrel that smelled like Arethusa Monk's father's cellar the time the home brew exploded.

In years to come, Dittany's fondest memory of that meeting would be the sight of Andrew McNaster trying to withdraw his overstuffed form quietly from the auditorium under cover of the furor.

Perhaps some of the other candidates got to speak their pieces. If so nobody remembered or gave a hoot. All were jittering on the edges of their chairs, breathless for the moment when Samantha Burberry confronted Sam Wallaby on the platform and explained why she'd come looking like a chimney sweep.

The moderator, realizing after a while that the others weren't getting a fair shake and being pretty itchy for the details himself, moved them up on the program and, out of gallantry, gave Samantha first chance to speak. She'd had no time to read over the speech Dittany had written for her but that fact bothered her not at all. By now the rescue, the hot soup, the tea, the buns, and the look on Sam Wallaby's face had restored her usual aplomb. It was a confident Samantha Burberry who stepped to the microphone.

"I apologize for appearing before you in this condition," she began, "but I had no time to change. Since I understand you've all been out looking for me, and I want to thank you here and now for your wonderful efforts, I don't have to tell you that I've been kidnapped since about ten o'clock last night. Sergeant Mac-Vicar and some kind friends found me only about half an hour ago, tied up and gagged in John Architrave's coalbin."

Naturally that news caused an outbreak of gasps and babbling. Samantha held up her hand for silence.

"Please bear with me. As you can imagine, I'm wobbly on my legs and my throat's sore from that gag and I'm absolutely dying for a hot bath, so I'd like to make my remarks brief. You all know, of course, that John Architrave was found shot last week up on the Enchanted Mountain with an arrow in him that nobody's been able to identify. I have no idea how that happened. I can only point out to you that my assailant, whom I can't identify, took me to poor old John's house for hiding. Whether you choose to draw any connection between those two facts is up to yourselves."

A buzz of connections surged through the hall. The moderator whanged his gavel. Samantha took a sip of the tea she'd brought to the podium with her and found voice enough to go on.

"As you also know, John Architrave was up on the mountain that day evidently because he'd ordered percolation tests to be done for a reason that has not been officially established. His death did serve one useful purpose. It focused attention on one of Lobelia Falls's most valuable natural resources; one, I may say, that has been grossly neglected by previous Development Commissions. Perhaps having some open land where our children can see wildflowers that have been wiped out elsewhere by the so-called progress of ill-managed urbanization doesn't seem important to some people. Not so important as putting a lot of town money and effort into a high school annex that somehow wound up in the hands of a private business, for instance. Not so important as defacing our main street by the removal of some fine old trees in order to create a parking lot that attracts litter and riffraff."

Loud cries of "You tell 'em, Samantha" led by Zilla Trott

prevented her from continuing until she again had to plead for silence.

"Some of us less imaginatively endowed citizens have never quite understood the alchemy by which town property gets diverted to the particular interests of certain individuals. A group became quite reasonably alarmed at the prospect of such a thing's happening in the case of the Hunneker Land Grant and urged me to offer myself as a write-in candidate for the Development Commission because they know I stand squarely on the side of maintaining public lands for the use of all our citizens instead of a privileged minority. The fact that so many have turned out to help turn the Enchanted Mountain into a workable park leads me to believe that the town as a whole feels the same way as I do."

"Damn right we do," bellowed Roger Munson, of all people, and an *a capella* chorus from all over the hall assured the speaker that Roger was damn well damn right they damn well did, too. Samantha took another sip of tea.

"Ever since I announced my candidacy last week, there have been attempts at harassment. Some were minor, like taking down my campaign posters. There was that episode of the goat let loose at the bake sale, which many of you witnessed. Late Saturday night a scene was staged up at Lookout Point that was obviously meant to suggest that the park we're trying to create would become a haven for rowdyism. Thanks to the truly heroic efforts of certain persons and one very brave dog, the vandals were caught in the act and chased away, but not before they had left a good deal of telltale evidence. This evidence was examined, photographed, tested and impounded by Sergeant MacVicar, who was at the scene of the crime only a few minutes after it happened, and I think we should all be proud and glad that we have such a vigilant officer heading our police force. And now I'd like to ask Sergeant MacVicar to come up here and tell you what these trash barrels full of broken beer bottles are all about because I'm really afraid I'm about to—"

As Samantha collapsed, so did Sam Wallaby's chances of getting elected. Dittany didn't wait to see him booed off the stage, as Zilla Trott later reported. Sergeant MacVicar was just advancing to the front of the auditorium when she helped Ben, Osbert, and Arethusa Monk, who had fallen temporarily into the role of Florence Nightingale, carry the still supine Samantha out of the hall and back to her own house.

By the time she got home, Samantha had revived enough to get her clothes off and have a bath and shampoo under Dittany's supervision while Arethusa heated up some of the leftovers from the party for which Samantha said her heart had been lusting during the lucid periods of her incarceration. While she was sitting up in bed getting her hair fixed by Dittany and eating from the dainty tray Arethusa had prepared, Joshua phoned. He asked how she was. She told him she'd spent almost the entire period of his absence bound and gagged in Mr. Architrave's coal cellar. Her husband laughed at this merry flight of fancy, told her several things she didn't particularly want to know about the conference, wished her luck on election day, said he'd be back in time to vote for her if he had to get out and push the plane all the way, and hung up. Samantha smiled fondly, finished the last bite on her tray, made dainty use of her serviette, lay down, and went to sleep.

Tuesday morning when the polls opened, those of the Grub-and-Stakers who had positioned themselves nearby with signs urging people to write in votes for Samantha Burberry were almost trampled underfoot by townsfolk champing at the bit to get into the polling booths and do just that. By noon, unofficial surveys indicated that Wallaby had been pounded to a gory pulp. Even before all the votes were counted, the verdict was so official it was ridiculous.

Andy McNasty was not going to get his Astroturf lawn with the pink plastic flamingo up on Lookout Point. God was in His heaven, all was right with Lobelia Falls, and everybody immediately concerned was over at Dittany Henbit's, naturally, getting sloshed. Sergeant MacVicar, accompanied on the melodeon by Mrs. MacVicar, was singing "Hail to the Chief" in the original Gaelic. Joshua Burberry, having reached home in the nick of time to cast his unneeded vote and absorb the realization that his wife had in truth been kidnapped and kept prisoner in the late John Architrave's coal cellar, was clutching Samantha rather ferociously to his side and thinking it might be a far, far better thing if Sergeant MacVicar would quit singing and go catch the kidnapper. Being a philosopher by profession, however, Joshua realized that it would do no good to say so because to all things there is a time and a season and any effort to hurry a Scot who had already announced his intention of rendering "Annie Laurie" as an encore would be futile.

Even Ethel was celebrating. The Binkles had brought her a beef bone to chew on. All and sundry were scratching her neck and thumping her backside and telling her what a great old mutt she was. However nobody, not even the Binkles, was inviting her to fetch her teddy bear and jammies and spend a night or two. Dittany had begun to realize she'd acquired herself a dog.

She was beginning to realize something else, too, and so were a good many of her guests. Ben Frankland was behaving toward her in a manner that could only be termed proprietary. To the trained observer it was clear that Hazel Munson was already thinking in terms of petits fours with pink and white icing for the linen shower and wondering if Dittany and Ben could get on with it in time for a June wedding because then Ben would be able to occupy his spare time during the summer painting the house, a task one could reasonably expect from a husband but not a paltry fiancé and goodness knew something had to be done about those peeling clapboards before another winter or the place would go to rack and ruin.

Dittany fully appreciated the convenience of having somebody around to fix the drinks and bring out the extra chairs, but she did wish he wouldn't be so free with remarks like "We ought to keep more ice in the fridge" and "We've been talking about remodeling the kitchen." Osbert Monk was glowering from behind the coal stove and hitching angrily at his trousers, which were still being held up by a tastefully knotted bit of clothesline. No doubt it seemed to him as it did to her that Ben was taking one heck of a lot for granted on the strength of a mutual enthusiasm for Fig Newtons.

Just to show everybody she was no pushover, Dittany went over and began chatting with Osbert about the distinction between an Apache and a Comanche. He was not altogether clear on the subject though he did confess that he'd always been secretly on their side even when the exigencies of his trade led him in a contrary direction. That got them on to the technicalities of writing, about which Dittany knew a great deal because Arethusa knew so little. She thought it would be only decent to show him how she'd organized her office and that this might be a good time because everybody else was clustered around Dot Coskoff's husband, who was doing his imitation of Nelson Eddy and Jeanette MacDonald to the usual tumultuous applause. She'd had enough tumult already to last her awhile, and Osbert was rather a cozy sort of person to talk to when there was nobody around for him to glower at.

All at once she said, "Osbert, if you were to buy this house, what would you do about it?"

"Do about it?"

"You know, fix it up. Remodel the kitchen and that sort of thing."

"But why should I want to? I mean," he blushed furiously, "I guess I could buy it if you needed some money or anything because if you write enough westerns you make quite a lot and I never seem to be able to think of anything to spend it on except that I've got to buy myself a new belt pretty soon because this clothesline is getting sort of frayed. I mean, if you happened to care to consider—well, maybe not an outright sale but a—well, I suppose you could call it a—that is, for instance if you and I—but what I mean is, why remodel the kitchen? What's wrong with the way it is?"

"You wouldn't be interested in tearing out the pantry, for instance?"

"Good gosh, no! If you haven't got a pantry, how can you keep one of those big old stone crocks in it full of molasses cookies about the size of dinner plates with sugar sprinkled on top?"

"Not hermits?"

"Hermits?" Osbert pondered the question. "You mean big, fat, spicy ones with lots of raisins in them?"

"Those were what I had in mind."

"Gee, I never thought of hermits. I mean, I was sort of hung up on molasses cookies the size of dinner plates with little gritty pieces of sugar sprinkled on top so they'd kind of crunch when you chewed them."

"And crinkly edges?"

"Well, naturally crinkly edges. So you could bite off the crinkles one by one before you really got to work on the cookie. On the other hand, though, there's a lot to be said for hermits. Dittany, I tell you what I'd do with this house if it were mine." Osbert's attractive hazel eyes shone with sudden inspiration. "What I'd do is, I'd get two of those big stone crocks, one for molasses cookies and one for hermits. Only I—well, you see, the problem is I don't know how to cook anything but bacon and eggs and I can't even do that without breaking the yolks more often than not. So that means I'd need somebody to—"

"Hey, Dittany! What are you doing in here, for Pete's sake? Can't you find something better to do? And we need more ice."

Ben Frankland was looking extremely put out.

"Then somebody will have to go someplace and get some," said Dittany, feeling more than a bit miffed herself. "We've already bummed from the Binkles, the Munsons, the Burberrys, the MacVicars, and Minerva Oakes. What about your Aunt Arethusa, Osbert?"

"Yeah," said Frankland, "what about your Aunt Arethusa, Monk? Why don't you go see if you can scare up some ice? Take your time."

"I'll be as quick as I can," said Osbert, and left.

"He needn't hurry on my account," said Ben. "I don't see why you had to hole up in here with a guy like him anyway. Now with a guy like me—"

"I'd better see what's happening in the kitchen," Dittany interrupted. "Is there anything left to eat?"

"Mrs. Binkle ran home and got some stuff, and the last I saw of Mrs. Munson she was putting together some kind of concoction with baked beans and chutney. Come to think of it, I was supposed to ask if you have any curry powder. Sounds God-awful, eh?"

"Hazel couldn't possibly make anything that wasn't delicious.

She cooks the way Arethusa Monk writes. You think it's going to be ghastly and everyone goes crazy about it."

"Jeez, I'll be glad when that creep nephew heads for the wide open spaces again," said Ben with feeling. "How much longer does he plan to stick around?"

"He hasn't said. I don't know why he should leave at all, if it comes to that. His aunt has an enormous house to herself, and two can write as cheaply as one, I expect. Personally, I'm hoping he stays. Maybe he'll throw a little business my way."

"Looks to me as if he's already throwing a little business your way," Frankland grunted. "What was that line he handed you about the cookie jars in the pantry?"

"You mean to tell me you've been eavesdropping again?" gasped Dittany.

"Now don't get up on your high horse, eh? I just happened to overhear a few words as I came looking for you about the curry powder."

"I thought it was about the ice."

"Well, it was, only I meant to mention the curry powder too. Now look, Dittany, you're just about the sweetest little kid I've ever run into, but when it comes to business you sure need somebody to give you a hand. For one thing, those writers are nothing but out-and-out moochers. The aunt comes sponging on you all the time and now the other one's started in at the same game. And furthermore you don't seem to realize that you're sitting on a valuable piece of residential property here. I'll admit this house is pretty much of a wreck now, but with a little cheap paint and wallpaper and maybe some nice green aluminum siding on the outside we could fix it up to look darn desirable. Only you've got to do something about a decent kitchen because that's what the women always fall for. Say we take out a little mortage to finance the renovations, we'd raise the market value by maybe two, three hundred per cent and sell out for—"

"Excuse me, Ben, I must look after my other guests."

Dittany was, after all, a Henbit and a Henbit did not breach the code of hospitality by laying out a guest under her own roof with an iron frying pan even when he used words like "sell out." And she hoped he'd noticed her use of the singular pronoun.

CHAPTER 20

As was only to be expected in Lobelia Falls, Dittany found when she circulated through the throng with Hazel's dip (which was, of course, superb) that the conversation had got around to archery. Now that Andy McNasty's hash was well settled and Sam Wallaby given his comeuppance, attention could be focused on more important matters like the Grand Free-for-All.

The interesting thing about the Free-for-All was that everybody competed against everybody else regardless of age, sex, or which branch of the Methodist Church they belonged to. The results always had the charm of unexpectedness. One year the gold ribbon had been won by Grandfer Coskoff, aged ninety-six at the time and since remarried; once by Zilla Trott shortly after she'd discovered wheat germ; once by a brigadier general in the Salvation Army; once by Hazel Munson's brother Euonymus Busch when a mere twig of ten and a quarter. Sam Wallaby had won twice although it was now being bruited about that he must have finagled his scores and needn't think he could get away with it again, eh.

"Well, I guess you'll have to include me out of that match," said Ben Frankland, who was still being the perfect host regardless of Dittany's rebuff. "I don't even know which end of a bow is up."

"Nor does anybody else," Sergeant MacVicar informed him with all gravity. "By the very nature of its symmetry a bow does not have its ups and downs like us frail creatures here below but will function well in almost any position, vertical or horizontal. The longbow is a far more versatile weapon than many people think. In essence, you see, it works on the same principle as the catapult, an ancient weapon much favored by the Greeks and Romans for the firing of burning arrows and other projectiles such as large stones over fortifications otherwise impenetrable. In the form of a slingshot the catapult is still employed by naughty little boys and sometimes, I fear, by naughty little girls."

He smiled benignly at Minerva Oakes. She was a crackerjack with a rubber band and a prune pit, as many a bluejay trying to swipe bird seed from a flock of feeding juncos and redpolls had learned to the detriment of its tail feathers. Osbert Monk, who had completed his ice-procurement mission on the double so that he could get back to exchanging glowers with Ben Frankland, nodded and made a note on his shirt cuff with an indelible pen. Dittany thought what hell it must be to marry a writer, even one who had sound views on pantries and needed somebody to bake him molasses cookies with crinkles around the edges. She wrenched her mind off the way Osbert's hair swirled around behind his left ear and attended to Sergeant MacVicar's learned discourse.

"That same principle of using the bow like a catapult was called into play," he was saying, "when our Dittany here and Mr. Benjamin Frankland were ostensibly shot at by John Architrave's murderer."

"Huh?" said Ben.

"Oh yes. That was another piece of Deputy Monk's detection. The method was simple enough. The bow, you see, was braced in the limbs of a tree by three hooks that held it in cocked position. Being without leaves at this time of year, the tree would present no obstacle to the passage of an arrow."

"Osbert figured that out in his own little pointed head?" cried Arethusa Monk.

"I used the idea in a book once," her nephew admitted modestly. "Anyway, I knew the tree had to be in a direct line with the one the arrow hit, and probably not too far away or else the fishline might get tangled up."

"What fishline, prithee?"

"The fishline he tweaked to release the bowstring and loose

the arrow. I expect he worked the same trick that night when he was supposed to be down cellar fixing Dittany's sump pump."

"He who?"

"Your astute nephew is referring to the man who prefers to be known as Benjamin Frankland," said Sergeant MacVicar.

"What do you mean, prefers to?" shouted Ben. "What are you getting at, eh?"

"You, myself, and the RCMP all know why you chose an alias which, by the way, sounds very much like an alias. As I mentioned to Dittany Henbit and Deputy Monk in your hearing last night, John Architrave's late sister has been traced. I thought you might make a run for it then, but you were too cocksure of your ability to pull the wool over a stupid small-town policeman's eyes. In point of fact, you would not have escaped. You have been under constant surveillance ever since you tipped your hand by faking that second attack on yourself and Dittany. Too much of a good thing can be very bad, Mr. Ford."

"Who's Mr. Ford?"

"You, sir. Your grandmother left one child who in turn married a man named Ford. Through diligence and ingenuity that might well have been turned to a worthier purpose, you are now the sole surviving member of that family. Your first name is Burton and you are well aware of growing property values in Lobelia Falls, as Dittany Henbit can testify, though in sober truth I do not believe any man who suggested tearing out her pantry could ever secure her affections and thereby her assets."

"Tearing out her pantry?" gasped Hazel Munson. "Is he crazy?"

"That is a defense he will perhaps try to offer, but it will not stand. Mr. Ford is merely the sort of person who distinguishes between *meum* and *tuum* only to the extent of determining how he can most expeditiously make yours become his. He is sometimes rather clever about this, as when he elected to conceal his relationship to John until he had not only got John safely out of the way but had ingratiated himself with the community. I daresay there might under different circumstances have been wide rejoicing when this helpful, friendly chap learned to his well-feigned astonishment that certain documents he would stumble across among his late grandmother's effects established him as John's long-lost heir."

Sergeant MacVicar took a delicate sip at his mild whiskey and water. "Yes. Mr. Ford is indeed a clever man. He is just never quite clever enough. That is why the RCMP happened to have on file the fingerprints my esteemed wife obtained when she, on whom I may say with pardonable pride there are no flies, offered him a drink of water when he dropped in at the station to make a fuss about our not having tracked down the imaginary hunter who allegedly shot his employer."

"Big deal," sneered Frankland. "They got me on a traffic violation once."

"True. You happened to be hijacking a truck at the time. What alerted Mrs. MacVicar, you see, was the map. She was well aware, as were we all, of poor old John's idiosyncrasy against maps and charts. Yet here was this new employee in possession of a plot plan allegedly given him by John and there was John dead on the mountain where in fact he had no need to be if in fact he had shown said employee the chart showing where to dig his totally irrelevant test holes."

"How do I know where the plan came from? All I know is Architrave gave it to me and told me to dig the holes. He must have got it from McNaster."

"McNaster would not have made a silly mistake like giving John a map. His research has been more thorough than yours, you see."

"What research? I don't know what you're talking about."

"Ah, but I do because my own research was even more thorough than McNaster's. You spent several days in Scottsbeck nosing around before you showed your face in Lobelia Falls. You found out your great-uncle was looking for a new man, as was so often the case. You also found out that McNaster had a scheme afoot with regard to the Hunneker Land Grant. Immediately you saw how this projected piracy could be turned to your own advantage."

"How, for instance?"

"You went to McNaster and pointed out that you had him, in a sense, over a barrel. However, if he would use his influence to get you the job with the Water Department, you would return the favor by falsifying the perk tests or doing other odd jobs for him. As a newcomer to the area, you would be in a favorable position to infiltrate the townsfolk and nose out any opposition to his plans. What you did not tell him, I dare say, was that, should your own plans go astray, you would make him the—I believe, Miss Monk, I would be correct in saying dupe or cat's-paw?"

"Right on the button, Sergeant, though you might also have used gull, scapegoat, whipping boy, or fall guy. I myself wouldn't say fall guy, of course, but—"

"Quite. In short, Mr. Ford, if pressed too far, you intended to accuse Andrew McNaster outright of shooting John Architrave."

"And what makes you so sure he didn't?"

"The fact that you and not he are John's heir, for one thing. The fact that the clerk who sold you the bow and arrows in that sporting goods store over at Scottsbeck has identified you from one of the photographs we took Saturday night after you'd organized Wallaby and his henchmen into staging that vandalism scene on the mountain. There is the fact that you used Mrs. Oakes's favorite brush to paint those black stripes on your arrows and neglected either to clean the brush or to wipe your fingerprints from the handle, as we discovered while searching her woodshed yesterday. In the matter of searching, there is the fact that you attempted to deceive Dittany, Mr. Monk, and myself by claiming that John's house had been searched to no avail and then offering to search the cellar by yourself. Had you done so, Samantha Burberry would of course not have been found in time to make her momentous appearance at Candidates' Night although, to give them their due, I believe that McNaster and Wallaby would have insisted on your releasing her afterward. Unlike yourself, they draw the line at out-and-out murder. Finally, of course, there is the fact that you neglected to order that gasket for Dittany's sump pump after you had said you would do so. *Falsus in uno, falsus in omnibus.*"

"I don't have to listen to this garbage," shouted Burton Ford.

Bob and Ray, who had been hovering at the ready, moved to his side. "It's not polite to contradict Sergeant MacVicar," said Ray.

"The hell it's not. What is this, Russia? Now you look here, MacVicar—"

His protest was cut short by the snapping of handcuffs.

CHAPTER 21

"The accused was about to get violent," Bob explained. "Can I charge him, Sarge? I never get to charge anybody."

"You'd louse up the words and let the bugger get off on a technicality," Ray objected.

"That will do, lads," said their chief benignly. "To continue my narrative, I was about to mention that these stalwart young men along with Deputy Monk have done some fine detective work."

"In the bars over at Scottsbeck, I'll bet," said Roger Munson.

"Exactly, and a happy hunting ground it proved to be. Our lads managed to contact (a) the young woman from the county surveyor's office who sold Frankland the map, (b) the chap who owned the van with the Manitoba number plates and his accomplices, all of whom had been contacted by Ford in his guise as Frankland working for McNaster through Wallaby, if I am not being too obfuscative. These three have already been charged with various things like trespass, vandalism, and the abduction of a goat. They appeared confident at the time of their arrest that a smart lawyer would soon get them out on bail. At last report, they were still waiting in vain for their deliverance."

"Charlie must have finked out," said Dittany. "He said he didn't want to be involved." As everybody present had heard her story of the invasion of McNaster's office in strictest confidence, they all looked knowing and said nothing.

"Mr. Monk also contacted a young woman from this area who had become, as it were, socially acquainted with Mr. Frankland and been providing him with information useful to his dire purpose."

"I'd have said fell design," said Arethusa Monk. "Do you mean to tell me my little Osbert waltzed himself into a bar and picked up a *broad?*"

Osbert's ears turned purple as the bloom on the sage. "It's not so hard, actually, once one gets the knack. Bob and Ray taught me how. In line of duty, needless to say."

"Well, stap my garters! So then what happened?"

"I bought her a Singapore sling and we chatted of this and that."

"Why a Singapore sling?"

"Because that's what she told me she wanted. I was endeavoring to ingratiate myself, you see. Bob and Ray had emphasized the importance of getting off on the right foot with a—that is, when engaged in detection. Anyway, I'd been looking for somebody connected with Lobelia Falls and she said she was, sort of, and I started mentioning people I'd met here and it turns out she happens to be related to somebody who knows you, Dittany. Though perhaps not very well," he added tactfully.

"Must have been that niece of Mrs. Poppy's she's always bending my ear about. Petunia, isn't it? Calls herself Petsy or something equally ridiculous. Forty-inch bust and a Dolly Parton wig?"

"She did appear to have a great deal of hair and—er—so forth."

"Especially the so forth," Ray put in with more enthusiasm than was warranted from an officer in pursuit of his duty. Sergeant MacVicar gave him a look. Osbert was allowed to continue without further interference from the Force.

"The gist of it is, I found Petsy had become what you might call friendly with Frankland—I mean Ford—and filled him in on a lot of stuff about Lobelia Falls. That's how he knew Mrs. Oakes had a room for rent. He must have been tickled stiff about that because he'd know from his grandmother that she was connected with his family by marriage. I'm sure Petsy also told him that Mrs. Oakes is a remarkably good shot with a bow and arrow for a—"

"If you're about to say for a woman her age, stuff it, Osbert," snapped Arethusa. "Half the women in this room are somewhere around Minerva's age and we're none of us any slouches. Okay, so what you're blethering about is that Minerva was slated to become this varlet's second-string dupe or cat's-paw in case his scheme to lay the blame on McNaster didn't work, eh?"

"That would be a reasonable assumption, Aunt Arethusa."

"The hell it would," Frankland/Ford started to protest, but Bob and Ray closed in and he decided he wasn't going to talk any more until he'd seen his lawyer.

"Anyway," said Osbert, "as we all know, Mrs. Oakes is a very sociable lady. I'm sure he found her a useful source of information."

Such as the fact that Miss Dittany Henbit owned her valuable residential property free and clear. Dittany thought of all the Fig Newtons this impostor had conned her out of and felt like crawling under the melodeon. Then she realized by some telepathic rapport that Osbert was thinking of them too, and looking very much as if he'd like to give the *soi-disant* Ben Frankland a punch in the mouth. She must remember to ask Arethusa for the Monks' old family recipe for large molasses cookies with crinkles around the edges and sugar on top.

As she was making that mental note she happened to catch Osbert's eye and blushed. Osbert blushed back. Hazel Munson, who had been in obvious distress at the prospect of not getting to frost pink cakes for the bridal shower, became quietly happy again. To be sure, Osbert would be no good whatever at painting the house or fixing the sump pump, but he did make lots of money being Lex Laramie. The older Munson boys needed to earn money for college and were skilled at all sorts of handyman jobs, so this would really be a much better arrangement all around. And of course it wouldn't have done for Dittany to marry a murderer.

"I wonder why he made all that fuss with the fishline, though," Hazel said aloud. "What if nobody had come along to see it happen when he shot off the arrow?"

"Oh, Frankland would have been pretty sure somebody would be there sooner or later," said Osbert. "Mrs. Oakes must have mentioned that she and Mrs. Trott and"—he almost said "Dittany" but blushed again and apparently decided the name was too precious to be uttered lightly—"and—and other people often walked on the mountain. I expect he told Mrs. Oakes enough to whet her curiosity about his doing perk tests up there and assumed that she herself would be the one to show up. That would have fitted beautifully into his plan about maybe getting her accused of shooting Mr. Architrave."

"Ben did tell me at breakfast and I was curious and I did mean to go," Minerva admitted. "Naturally I wondered what blooper poor old John was about to commit this time, but to tell you the truth I didn't take it very seriously. I thought Ben would probably get down to the office and John would forget to show up and tell him where to dig. I didn't know about the plot plan, you see. If Ben had told me about that, I'd have smelled a rat right then and there because I may be a fool but I'm not a damn fool, as my father used to say. Anyway Zilla and I had planned to work on our hooked rugs in the morning, then we had our club meeting in the afternoon. What with one thing and another, it slipped my mind and I never got around to going."

"It was a piece of luck for Frankland or Ford or whatever his name is that Dittany happened along," Zilla observed.

"Yes, Dittany couldn't have been more perfect. I mean not so perfect that a chap would ever find her monotonous to be with, but—I mean, I know you're not supposed to say more perfect because perfect either is or it isn't, but—"

"But Dittany made an ideal witness to Ford's trick," Sergeant MacVicar kindly interposed, "thus providing him with what appeared to be an excellent alibi. Quite unintentionally, to be sure."

"Well, naturally," said Osbert. "I mean it would appear natural that any man would wish to shield such a rare flower of youth and beauty from any and all perils, particularly arrows whizzing past her adorable little noggin. Ford was doing no more than a woman might reasonably expect—I mean a woman like Dittany—I mean, oh, heck, you know what I mean. Like that it wouldn't look odd or unexpected for him to shove her in behind the backhoe out of harm's way and tell her to stay there while he went and did his fake chest-thumping act, making believe he was facing deadly peril and all that garbage when in fact he was hiding the bow and rolling up the fishline.

"After he'd got the evidence hidden, he pretended to discover Mr. Architrave's body, which of course he knew perfectly well had been there all the time. He himself had shot Mr. Architrave while they were wandering around looking for spots to dig perk test holes. He'd have been better off to wait till Mr. Architrave picked a spot because, from what I can gather, the old man, however dumb he might have been, would never have been stupid enough to dig up the only patch of Spotted Pipsissewa in Lobelia County."

"That is a telling point, Mr. Monk," said Sergeant MacVicar. "John was perhaps not a particularly quick man, nor indeed a particularly wise man, but he was a fundamentally decent man. Moreover, he was a man who had intimate personal acquaintance with every inch of land in Lobelia Falls. John would have known where the Spotted Pipsissewa grew. He would not have countenanced its being disturbed, molested, or uprooted despite the fact that he had allowed himself to be duped, gulled, or perhaps I should say catspawed by Andrew McNaster into doing percolation tests at the wrong time of year on land where no tests should have been done at all."

"I wonder how McNaster managed that," mused Roger Munson.

"We believe John was persuaded by means of a spurious legal document prepared by a member of the legal profession from Scottsbeck who is, I fear, no credit to his time-honored profession and will, I trust, prove but a broken reed when Mr. Ford retains him as counsel in the hope of escaping the just penalty for his heinous and perfidious crime. Mr. Ford, I am now going to charge you formally with the murder of John Architrave. I shall ask Miss Dittany Henbit to take down the exact verbiage of my charge in her excellent shorthand while each member of this assemblage pays careful attention. As my capable assistant pointed out a moment ago, we wish to leave no legalistic loophole through which you may able to effect an escape."

Thereupon Sergeant MacVicar proceeded to charge Burton Ford, alias Benjamin Frankland, as thoroughly as any prisoner has ever been charged. Dittany typed her shorthand notes in triplicate and passed the transcriptions around for everybody to read and sign, which everybody did in due order. The prisoner was led to the patrol wagon. En route he most injudiciously took a swipe at Osbert Monk. Mr. Monk was thus forced in self-defense, as everybody clamored to testify, to land a right to Ford's jaw that left Bob and Ray gazing back at him in awe and reverence even as they dragged their captive away.

Mrs. MacVicar, who had been unable to suppress a beam of wifely adoration as she watched her husband so nobly acquit himself in his official duty, recovered her wonted dignity and thanked Dittany for a lovely evening. She again congratulated Samantha on her triumph at the polls, expressed proper sentiments anent public servants and their responsibilities to the citizenry they represented, and took her leave.

Gradually the guests drifted off, Minerva Oakes being comforted by Zilla Trott on the loss of yet another boarder and yet another betrayal of her hospitality and being told for the cat's sake never to rent that room again until the applicant had been screened by some method other than Minerva's own totally unreliable intuition. Samantha and Joshua stayed until the last, shaking every hand offered with true political finesse. Then they both kissed Dittany and went home.

"Good heavens," Dittany remarked to Ethel, "we're alone. How strange!"

Then she heard a diffident cough from the pantry.

"Er—Dittany?"

"Osbert! I thought you'd gone off with Arethusa."

"I—er—came back. I thought I'd just like to—er—visualize how those two cookie crocks might look. Side by side, that is. I mean, close together. I mean"—Osbert hitched up his clothesline, took a few deep breaths, and clasped Dittany to his manly bosom —"like this."

"Osbert," Dittany murmured into his shirt front, "about this house. Would you really like to live here?"

"Is there a better place?"

"You're quite sure you wouldn't want to change anything?"

"Only the name on the mailbox," he cried with a romantic fervor even Sir Percy would have been hard put to emulate. "Oh, Dittany!"

First timidly, then boldly, his lips explored the little dimple at the corner of her mouth. "Did anybody ever tell you your cheek is like the bloom on the yucca or Spanish bayonet?"

From somewhere far, far away a voice could have been heard to remark, "Well, stap my garters!"

Dittany and Osbert heeded not the voice. Arethusa could go stap her own garters. They had far more interesting things to do.

In Aprille with his shoures soote, Hazel got to frost little pink and white cakes. In May, Gram Henbit's wedding dress was shaken out of its blue tissue paper wrappings and a very jittery young author bought himself a new belt. In June, the Munson boys were hired to paint a house. And thus (as Chaucer and Miss MacWilliams might have wound up the tale) with alle blisse and melodye, hath Osbert Monk y-wedded Dittany.